Little Drops of Blood

Also by Bill Knox

LITTLE DROPS OF BLOOD

Bill Knox

Constable · London

First published in Great Britain 1962
This edition published in Great Britain 2000
by Constable, an imprint of Constable & Robinson Ltd
3 The Lanchesters, 162 Fulham Palace Road
London W6 9ER
Copyright © 1962 Bill Knox
The right of Bill Knox to be identified as the author of
this work has been asserted by him in accordance with
the Copyright, Designs and Patents Act 1988

ISBN 0-094-804109

Printed and bound in Great Britain

A CIP catalogue record for this book is available from the
British Library

For Alistair

CHAPTER ONE

Occurrence report. Constable Matthew MacDonald, Car One-Five, Traffic Department.

Following radio message received from Control, timed 23.48 hours, Thursday, April 22, proceeded to South Salisbury Road where beat constable was already in attendance. Deceased civilian was lying on west side of the roadway at a point of fifteen yards north of engine factory entrance. Patrol radioman John Murray assisted beat constable in search for witnesses. None located. Roadway poorly lit at locus. On preliminary examination, deceased appeared to be victim of traffic accident. Multiple injuries, and clear traces of car treads on raincoat. Second inspection of area, however, showed indications which decided me to request C.I.D. attendance. Detective Inspector Moss of Millside Division arrived at locus at 00.29 hours.

Phil Moss shivered, thought wistfully of the thick woollen cardigan hanging on a peg in his office, and dug his hands deeper into the pockets of his baggy tweed suit. The hour after midnight on an April morning in Scotland is not the best for thoughts of spring.

"Sorry to drag you out, Colin," he apologised. "But when I got here and saw what MacDonald meant, well, it was obviously time to pass the job up the line."

"Forget it." Chief Detective Inspector Colin Thane, head

of Millside Division C.I.D., pushed his grey felt hat a couple of inches further back on his forehead and took in the scene. The traffic patrol car stood a few feet away, its dipped headlights trained on the section of roadway where an anonymous shape, now decently covered by an old grey blanket, lay in a formless huddle. The blanket wasn't quite large enough for the task. A foot protruded from one edge, a white area of flesh visible marking the gap between sock and trouser leg.

South Salisbury Road was deserted. Little more than an industrial alleyway, it was flanked on the west side by a high red brick wall which acted as a barricade between the road and the almost parallel railway tracks. Beyond lay a network of sidings, one of Glasgow's main goods traffic marshalling yards. Somewhere in the distance, carried clear on the frosty air, he could hear the panting purr of a diesel locomotive, punctuated by the clatter of buffers as the task of late-night shunting went ahead. On the east side of the tarmac surface the black, empty bulk of an engine factory loomed in the air, flanked on either side by other anonymous industrial structures. There was a night watchman in the engine building. But he'd heard nothing, seen nothing.

"I've put a man fifty yards down the road in each direction," volunteered Moss. "There isn't likely to be traffic moving through at this hour but, well, I thought we'd better seal off the place." He shivered again.

"Feeling it cold, Phil?" Thane grinned from the insulation of his heavy overcoat. "You know the saying, 'Never cast a cloot till May's oot.'"

His second in command grunted. "It's been warm for the last three days. How was I to know we were going back to winter tonight?" He shuffled his feet. "Where'd you want to start?"

"Better have a look at him first," said Thane. "Any identification yet?" They walked into the pool of light, over towards the blanket, careful to keep beyond the white chalk line drawn round an area of the roadway's tarmac.

Moss shook his head. "No papers in his pockets. Some keys, money, a penknife, a few other odds and ends. That's all. But I've seen his face somewhere. At least, I think I have. It's—well, a bit difficult."

Gently, Thane lifted one corner of the blanket, winced, and replaced it slowly. "It doesn't help," he agreed. One wheel of the car must have passed over the lower half of the man's face. The upper portion was clear of blood and surprisingly undamaged. But the crushed area had been twisted into a grotesque nightmare. He turned away. "Where's MacDonald?"

"Sir?" The uniformed man, anticipating the summons, was standing almost at his elbow. Constable MacDonald was a heavy, craggy Highlander, a slow-spoken, deliberate type of cop who'd been on patrol cars since they first started fooling around with a toy called two-way mobile radio.

"You've turned up a good one this time," said Thane grimly. "Where are they?"

"Over here a wee bit, sir." Careful of the chalk barrier line, the two detectives followed him a few paces along the roadway. MacDonald added the beam of his hand-torch to the patrol car's glare, then crouched down and pointed. Small, red, more frozen than congealed, the drops of blood formed a trail at irregular intervals. Each drop was circular in shape, except where a small jagged edge pointed north, away from the dead man, down to where the road vanished into a line of twinkling street lights.

"And the others?" Thane rose from his knees and nodded in understanding as MacDonald led them back along the road again, past the blanket, stopping just short of the patrol car. Another trail of blood drops ran for a few feet. But this time the little jagged edge pointed south.

"That's it, sir. Except for the way he's been smashed up," said MacDonald. He hesitated, then plunged on. "We see plenty of hit-and-run bodies in this job. But this one—" he shook his head. "He's almost mangled."

Phil Moss cleared his throat. "There's what could be tyre marks on the road further up," he added. "But they're not clear enough to be much help."

"Thanks, sir." The patrol driver accepted the cigarette offered by Thane, found matches in his tunic pocket and gave a light to the two detectives. Then, true to his cautious Highland nature, he blew out the match, struck another, and lit his own cigarette. Third light avoided, he tucked both match ends back in the box.

Thane let a long trickle of smoke drift into the air. Frost was beginning to form on the patrol car's roof. The temperature must still be falling. "Work it out for us," he invited.

MacDonald took a moment or two before he began, choosing his words carefully. "I heard about it once, a long time ago—when cars used to drip a lot more oil than they do now. It went like this, sir. You could always tell the direction a car had been travelling from the way the oil-drops lay. It . . ." he frowned, searching for his explanation. "They fell two ways at once, if you know what I mean. Straight down because of gravity, but moving forward a bit because the car had been heading that way. That's how you get the little rough edge. Well, you expect blood around a traffic accident. If someone really gets bashed and goes under a car, then he could be dragged along for a bit, and that would account for a blood trail leading up to the body and away from it. The trail away could be due to dripping from the underside of the car."

Then he scowled emphatically. "But I've never seen a blood trail that pointed two ways before."

Thane nodded, and exchanged glances with Moss. The dead man had been killed by a car all right—but by a car which had driven over him, probably stopped a few yards beyond, then had deliberately reversed back over the body again. Nagging at the back of Thane's mind was the realisation that there was something lacking in the picture, something he still couldn't give a name. Anyway, they had a murder on their hands. He released his last faint hold on the long week-end fishing trip he'd been trying to wangle from days-off due.

"It could have been a hit-and-run driver who panicked," suggested Phil Moss hopefully.

"And ran back over him to finish the job off?" Thane's voice was heavy with disbelief. "Maybe that happened sometimes in the Middle East when there was a war on. But not any more, Phil. First thing we've got to find out is who he was. We'll run his fingerprints through records. That may help, if your hunch is right."

Headlights glowing, a car was approaching. It slowed and remained stationary at the police check point; then the motor revved again and the vehicle came on, to stop almost beside them. A man got out, lifted a small bag from the rear seat, and came over.

"Busy time tonight," said Doc Williams, the police surgeon, as he moved into the pool of light. "There's been a stabbing over in the Gallowgate. What have we here, Colin?" Without a pause, he prodded Moss in the chest with one long forefinger. "You look cold, Phil."

"Freezing." Moss shivered involuntarily, and hunched his shoulders.

Doc Williams chuckled, taking in the small, thin figure before him. "Well, you know the saying. 'Never cast a cloot . . .'"

"'Till May's oot,' I know," agreed his victim wearily. Phil Moss was beginning to cultivate an active dislike for the old Scots proverb and its chiding advice on the need for winter woollens.

The police surgeon pulled off his leather gloves, stuffed them into one pocket, and went over to the blanket. His bag on the roadway beside him, he squatted down, lifted the cloth, and gave a low whistle. "What hit him? A tank?"

"Don't move things around too much, Doc," warned Thane. "We're still waiting for the Scientific mob."

Doc Williams peered more closely at the corpse, clinical interest written large on his face. He took a small pencil-beam torch from his bag to aid the close-range examination. "There's a flask of coffee in my car," he remarked casually. "Fancy some when I'm finished?" At last he rose, shutting the bag with a snap. "That's it for the moment. Can't do a proper job until we move him, but I'd say he was killed instantly. Smashed rib cage and pelvis, multiple internal injuries—and, of course, the head. Probably happened about two hours ago."

Thane calculated. That meant half an hour or so before the beat constable made his initial discovery. A quiet industrial side street like this one was rarely used after darkness, and the nearest block of houses was several hundred yards distant, across the railway tracks.

Doc Williams was now over at the blood-drop trail, guided by Moss. He found it interesting. "You kept your eyes open, MacDonald," he acknowledged. The patrol man, still on guard by his discovery, came close to a blush of embarrassment. But his momentary confusion was overlooked as another vehicle rolled into the cordoned zone. The Scientific Bureau's mobile lab was a big, sand-coloured van which, from outward appearance, could have belonged to any one of half a dozen delivery firms in the city. Almost brand new, replacing a vehicle retired through sheer old age, it was the Bureau's current pride and joy. The barely run-in engine had more attention devoted to it on the average day than any child at a welfare clinic. Even as the Bureau detail headed towards Thane the van's driver nipped out, produced a large white duster, and began polishing away at a few specks of mud which had appeared on the nearside wing.

"This is a hell of an hour to drag out a man of my age," complained the hatless, shaggy-haired leader of the new arrivals. "Is it a good one?"

"Murder by motorcar," said Thane. He was more than a little relieved to see Dan Laurence had elected to come along. The Scientific Bureau superintendent, an untidy, portly, rough-tongued character who might have stomped straight from some backwoods farm, possessed a needle-sharp mind when it came to the forensic field. He was good, very good—though the suggestion would have appalled him.

"A car, eh?" growled Laurence. "Mmph. Well, it makes a change." He nodded to the police surgeon. "Got you along too, eh?" Then his eye lighted on Phil Moss. "And how's the wee Inspector?"

Moss mumbled noncommittally.

"Feelin' the cold, eh? Where's your coat, man? No' even a cardigan? Remember the saying . . ."

"He's already been told." Thane stepped in with a grin, intent on preventing a possible explosion.

"Aye, no doubt." The Scientific Bureau chief rubbed his hands vigorously. "If it gets any colder some brass monkeys are going to need a welding job, so help me." He turned to business. "What's the drill, Colin?"

Thane sketched the position in a few sentences. Laurence listened without interruption, then grunted understanding. He turned to his squad, three eager young detective constables, each laden with equipment. "Right, lads, here we go. Photos first, Willie. Johnny, give him a hand with the flash-gear. The body for a start, then some close-ups of those wee drops of blood. Make them nice and sharp now, Willie—or I'll hand you your guts on a plate."

Willie suppressed a smile, and gave the rest of the team a broad wink as he turned away. Laurence scratched his thatch of hair as he disposed of the last of the trio. "You'll need to take his fingerprints, Frank. No' a very nice job, I'm afraid. When you've got them . . ." he turned to Thane. "Eh, Colin, how about me borrowing one o' your cars to run a message? I'll get the prints sent straight back for a comparison check. There won't be much you can do about this till you find out who he was."

"It's yours when you're ready," agreed Thane.

Doc Williams stood silent, watching the police photographer assemble his camera and flash-gear. Then, in a quiet, emotionless voice, he broke in. "Dan, you'd better have him take a few close-up shots of the legs. Pictures that will show exactly how they're lying."

Like the others, Thane turned towards the police surgeon, openly puzzled.

Doc Williams remained impassive. "It could be important, Colin. This man wasn't knocked down. He was laid on the road before the car rolled over him. Probably unconscious."

Phil Moss sucked on his teeth. Even Dan Laurence showed surprise.

"You're sure?" demanded Thane.

The police surgeon nodded. "I'm sure. I've been thinking about it for the last few minutes. Look, Colin, if he'd been run down by any form of vehicle he'd have leg injuries. They always do—usually been slammed by the car bumper. There may or may not be broken bones, but there's always at least lacerations. His legs are undamaged."

The missing factor slid into place. Thane gave a snap

of his fingers. Now he realised what had been troubling him. A man had been knocked down. Yet nowhere on the road surface had he seen broken glass from a smashed headlight, paint fragments, scrape marks, or even underwing mud—inevitable traces, singly or in combination, after a vehicle and a human body come in impact.

Doc Williams stifled a yawn. "You've got yourself a case this time, Colin. A case and a half." He yawned again, openly this time. "Bed is calling. But it looks as if I can postpone that pleasure for a few hours. I'll wait until you move the body, then give it another look-over at the mortuary. After that the full post-mortem works can wait for a bit." A thought struck him. "Anyone interested in coffee?"

Divisional Chief Inspectors have, among other minor compensations of rank, their own private overnight suite. It consists of a folding camp bed and a washbasin, both contained within their police station office space. But by four A.M. the camp bed was still waiting and unoccupied —though Thane was at least one step further forward, he knew the identity of the body on his hands.

The night staff at the Headquarters fingerprint department had carried out a fast coding job on the inked impressions of the dead man's prints, then had begun sifting. They had 150,000 specimens on record, but the classification system cut down their task. A ten-print card from the two-handed collection could now be withdrawn from circulation.

Sammy Bell had been his name. The duty man at the Criminal Record Office along the corridor checked through the Bells on his list, found three with the first name "Samuel," double-checked on the C.R.O. number indexed on the ten-print card, and passed on the result.

Sammy hadn't been a specialist. Theft, fraud, and the occasional assault comprised the bulk of his history of previous convictions, which were considerable without being impressive. He had been thirty years of age, and had been released from Barlinnie Prison seven months previously at the end of his last sentence for housebreaking.

Phil Moss, still cold and now decidedly weary, searched out the one slender lead to Sammy's more recent background, the address listed under "Next of Kin."

The dead man's brother, still half-asleep when he answered the door at his top-floor tenement flat, expressed the bare minimum of emotion on hearing of his bereavement. Vince Bell was a plumber and, according to the local beat cop, was also an honest citizen.

"Sure, I'm sorry the poor basket's bought it," he grunted. "He was my own brother, wasn't he? But I tossed him out of that door almost two years ago when he tried to dip my wife's housekeeping. I'd had enough. I haven't seen or heard of him since, and that was how I wanted it."

Grudgingly, he agreed to pay a call at the mortuary and carry out formal identification. But there was a more practical worry on his mind. "Who's going to have to pay for the funeral, mate?"

Moss shrugged, left the question unanswered, and headed back to the heated warmth of Millside station. Perched on the desk in Thane's office, he told the story, then shook his head. "That's it, Colin. The well's gone dry."

Thane lit the last cigarette from his packet, felt the smoke raw and harsh in his throat, and promptly stubbed the tobacco into the half-full ash tray. "Leave it at that for now," he said, fighting his eyelids open by sheer muscular effort. "I've roughed the initial report for Headquarters, and there's damn all else I can think of right away. Get some sleep, Phil, but be back for nine. Oh, and on your way out tell the duty man to wake me when the shifts change over."

Moss nodded and went out. Alone in the room, Colin Thane glowered at the camp bed with a distaste born of experience. Still, three hours would be better than no sleep at all.

Divisional overnight reports were at C.I.D. Headquarters by eight A.M. At eight-twenty, even earlier than he'd anticipated, the telephone summons reached Thane's office. Fifteen minutes later, after a fast car journey from Millside to St. Andrew's Square, he reached the Headquarters building, left his driver there, and walked the few yards across the street to the Central Division building, where "Buddha" Ilford's office was located. They'd been waiting for him. Thane was ushered straight through, and moments later was sitting on one side of the broad desk, his eyes on the bulky figure facing him.

As usual, Ilford appeared in no hurry. With slow-motion ease he plugged a few final shreds of dark brown tobacco into the bowl of the latest aluminium-stemmed pipe, struck a safety match, and puffed until the red glow and smoke-clouds were to his satisfaction. The morning bundle of reports was piled before him, the Millside sheet on top.

"This patrol car man MacDonald used his head," he acknowledged. Which, from Chief Superintendent Ilford, was considerable praise. The head of Glasgow C.I.D. was not particularly given to unqualified comment. Some junior officers secretly wondered how he'd ever managed to accept the marriage ceremony without being able to temper the words "I do" into more cautious phraseology.

Thane always felt a little uncomfortable in the small ground-floor room, its walls lined with old-fashioned bookcases, a faded strip of carpet round the desk forming an island of nondescript grey on the dark brown linoleum. Too often a summons to Buddha's office could mean trouble in store for all concerned.

Across the desktop the Chief Superintendent seemed lost in the contemplative meditation which had earned him his nickname. He sucked a few more times on his pipe. "It's in your division, Colin. And it stays your case. But we can help you along the way. That's why I called you over." With a grunt he stretched down, riffled through the bundles of red cardboard folders lying on the floor beside his chair, selected one, and handed it over. "This is all yours now— though we've done little more than scrape the surface. What do you know about Sammy Bell?"

Thane shrugged, and rubbed his chin with one hand. At least he'd managed to shave before the call had come. "Not much more than what Records dug out for us. He'd never pulled a job in the Millside area, but he appears to have been bobbing in and out of jail most of his life."

Ilford gave a ponderous nod. "Occupation?"

"From the look of things, he probably hadn't done an honest day's work in years." Thane frowned. "I think they said he originally served an apprenticeship as a mechanic."

"Motor mechanic," agreed the Chief Superintendent. "And a good one too. Last time he was inside, he overhauled every piece of motorised equipment in the prison— including the governor's car. Seems it goes like a bomb now—they're going to miss him." He laid the pipe down on a massive glass ash tray. "Read the returns on stolen cars lately, Colin?"

Thane hadn't. A Divisional Chief Inspector seldom had time to keep up with the torrent of statistical offerings which poured in each week. And Millside had been having a busy month, including two major robberies and a gentleman with a new line in embezzlement patterns. He stayed hopefully silent.

Ilford was too engrossed in his subject to notice. "London's the worst area, of course. They're approaching the ten-thousand-vehicles-a-year mark." He felt it unnecessary to add that that meant an estimated three and a half million pounds' worth of transport being appropriated—even though five out of six vehicles were usually recovered relatively intact. "That's London's worry. But figures are climbing in our own parish, have been for months. Somebody's working hard on the hot car racket, Colin, and probably clearing a small fortune in the process. Sammy Bell looked like being our first lead. One of the ghost squad found him when he'd had just enough drink to be tongue-free. Sammy wasn't quite ripe for squealing, but he wasn't far from it. Our man gathered that Sammy wanted more cash for what he was doing, and that the boss of the setup wouldn't wear it." He sighed. "We decided to leave him alone for a day or two, and give him time to work up some more steam. Then this happens—blast it."

That, decided Thane, put a new complexion on the situation. Had Sammy been spotted by his comrades as a potential informer—or had he merely annoyed them to the point where he had to be removed from the scene?

Wood creaked as the Chief Superintendent levered himself from his chair. "Our one spot of luck is that the newspapers seem to have decided this was just another traffic accident. I want it to stay that way as far as reporters are concerned. Let this gang feel they're perfectly safe, that they've pulled it over us. That way, they're more likely to be careless. Oh, and there's no sense contacting the ghost squad man—every shred he knows is in his report." He glanced at the plain-fronted grandfather clock in one corner of the room. "I've an appointment with the Rotary Club in ten minutes' time. They're being shown round the building, then I've to give 'em a talk on crime prevention. Well, there's the file, Colin. Keep in touch."

Thane read the Headquarters file while the duty car took him back to his own division. The file was, to put it mildly, threadbare on fact and held together mainly by theory. When it concentrated on Sammy Bell, it was almost nonexistent. But it gave one definite lead he'd been needing. To outward appearances, at any rate, Sammy Bell had been working for a living. He'd been employed as a pump attendant and mechanic at a small filling station on the outskirts of the city, situated on the main road south. The petrol station was one of a group operated and owned by the Ascension Garage Company. Thane didn't run a car of his own, but he'd heard of Ascension, a firm with a pretty straight reputation, and one which held agencies for several leading British and Continental makes. Their main garage was a converted cinema—a cinema which lay only about half a mile away from South Salisbury Road where Sammy Bell had kept an appointment with death. Headquarters had made a quiet survey of the Ascension firm. Their verdict, somewhat unsurprisingly, was that there seemed no reason to suspect anything wrong there. The business was healthy and prosperous.

The duty car slowed and halted outside the main door of Millside police station. Thane pushed the papers back into their cardboard container, got out, and went straight up to his first-floor office. Phil Moss was there, and by some magical piece of timing the uniformed orderly appeared with two steaming mugs of tea.

"How was it?" queried Moss, strategically positioned beside the glowing two-bar electric fire.

Thane told him in detail, glad of a chance to express his feelings adequately before a sympathetic and private audience. When he finished, he took another long gulp of tea from the mug, and grimaced. "So we've to 'keep in touch.' In Buddha's dictionary, that stands for 'tidy this lot up, and don't be too long about it.'"

Detective Inspector Moss sipped his milky, weaker brew and launched his own rebellious contribution. "Millside is being asked to pull one of Headquarters' chestnuts out of the fire—a chestnut that's already been badly singed. Well, you couldn't say no, Colin—but we've still nothing much to go on. Dan Laurence phoned in ten minutes ago. His boys had another look around the roadway as soon as it was daylight, but found little fresh. They've identified the size of tyre from the marks it left on Sammy Bell and on the road. It was a five-ninety by fourteen, tubeless, according to the tread pattern. Could fit half a dozen makes of medium saloon, and there were no nonstandard peculiarities. They've started a spectroscopic check on Sammy's clothes—oh, and the post-mortem's going ahead. We'll get the results about noon." One hand dipped into his pocket, and reappeared with a slim glass tube. He shook two small pink pills on to his palm, put them in his mouth, and grimaced as he swallowed.

Thane ignored the performance. The size, shape, and colour of the pills altered from time to time, but Phil Moss and his ulcer were too firmly established in local lore to call for other than occasional comment. He frowned. "Where's our copy of the stolen car returns?"

"They've been filed. I'll get them." His second in command rose with a reproachful sigh, went over to one of the big filing cabinets in the room, and began searching. He knew Colin Thane's antipathy towards paperwork. In fact, apart from Thane's wife and two children, Phil Moss probably knew him better than anyone alive. It was six years now since they'd first teamed up. Thane, the younger man, had been transferred to take over the division. Moss, older, perhaps more conscious of routine, was drafted in from Headquarters to assist him owing to the outgoing chief inspector and his number two having reached retirement age almost within days of one another.

He found the lists, and brought them over.

Thane scanned the closely tabulated figures, a slight scowl on his face. In his early forties, just over the six-foot mark, dark-haired, built like a professional footballer though perhaps a shade too plump to be in perfect physical trim, he was indulging in a momentary bout of self-criticism. He should have read these returns. He knew the trend-indicating significance and importance of the charts and graphs and lists which flowed in on a score of different subjects. But there lay the dilemma when you were a cop. Which came first—having every possible background detail at your fingertips, or being out, tackling the crimes which built these same analytical cyphers? That, he mused, was where Phil became a double blessing. The thin, slightly built detective might have hypochondriacal tendencies when it came to his stomach and general health, and he was certainly far removed in appearance from the outsider's idea of a typical cop. For a start, there was the constant mystery surrounding how he'd squeezed past the entry medical, with its minimum height specification. But the very fact that Phil didn't look like a cop, combined with his seemingly tireless ability to digest small mountains of paperwork and still be handy in a back-street battle, made him a perfect running-partner.

He gave up, lit a cigarette, and shoved the packet across the desk. "Let's hear your version of these figures."

Moss helped himself, accepted a light, and coughed happily as the smoke invaded his lungs. "For a start, car-grabbing's on the increase. You know how it usually goes —more often than not a stolen car turns up pretty quickly. It's either been taken by some kids on a joy-riding spree, or by a bunch of neds who want transport for some house-breaking job. Then, of course, there's the specialist who strips off accessories, tyres, and battery, then dumps the remains. Whichever it is, most of these are found abandoned within twenty-four hours."

Thane doodled quietly on his deskpad, listening, filling in a little row of car outlines. Crooks didn't use the hire-and-drive system so often now. The underworld had caught on fast to the fact that many of the larger firms now had a hidden camera installed in their renting offices, taking a photographic record of each customer.

"And now, we've a change," he encouraged.

"Aye." Moss warmed to his subject. "The pattern's still the same in other cities. But not here, not any more. There's been an estimated twenty per cent increase in car stealing." He paused warily. "Headquarters returns show that the incidence graph began climbing about three months ago, and reached its peak four weeks past. Now it's remaining steady at the new rate—and the extra cars which disappear just don't show up again. The type of car that's vanishing is pretty significant, Colin. This bunch are concentrating on mass-production saloons, medium horsepower, never more than a year old. And they take no chances. Almost every car has been nobbled from some off-street parking lot near a business area or factory plant, and hasn't been reported stolen until hours later. Say the owner is on a nine-till-five job. That means the nobbler can have up to eight hours' clear start before the shouting begins."

"It figures." Thane abandoned the growing number of car sketches, each complete with driver, and tapped his pencil on the desk. "Whoever we're after is running this as something close to an organised business. Sammy Bell hinted that, and more. Our man hand-picks his cars for a fast resale, and concentrates on makes that are sure of a ready market."

At a minimum of five hundred pounds' profit per car, the returns were formidable, even though the vehicle would have to be dressed up a little—new registration plates, maybe even a change of tyres and a fresh paint job. But could it really be so easy?

"There's licencing and taxation," protested Phil, giving his answer to the same unspoken question. "Every car needs a registration book, right? Maybe they buy a few books picked up in house burglaries. Maybe they get a

few more by buying up scrapped cars—you know, an insurance write-off after a crash. But would they get enough
that way to support this kind of trade?"

Thane nodded. Selling the actual cars might be simple
enough, using either the small ad columns or making an
approach to an unsuspecting dealer. The Motor Taxation
office would have little chance of picking up every forgery
—but not all would have escaped them, and the Headquarters file made a point of noting that nothing unusual
had so far been spotted in that quarter.

He tossed the pencil down on the pad, and pressed the
buzzer switch fitted by the side of his desk. Out in the
main C.I.D. room, Sergeant MacLeod abandoned his expenses sheet, stubbed his cigarette, and a moment later
put his head round the corner of Thane's door.

"Want me, sir?"

Thane nodded. "Come in a minute, sergeant. How are
you fixed for work?"

Sergeant MacLeod grinned. "Shiney Lewis got eighteen
months at the Sheriff Court for the pawnbroker job. Paddy
Linn just phoned in from the court."

Shiney had decided to get into the pawnbroker's by cutting a hole through the roof. Unfortunately, he'd forgotten
to check that the place was empty at the time. The pawnbroker was doing a late-night stocktake, heard Shiney at
work, and Sergeant MacLeod and Detective Constable
Linn had been waiting below when the uninvited visitor
dropped down into the darkened pawn office.

"Keep him out of the road for a bit, anyway," said
Thane. "Anything else?"

MacLeod shook his head. "Just that television maintenance fraud, sir."

Phil Moss gave a groan. "Not another one?"

"Usual," agreed MacLeod. "Pay me so much cash down

and I'll look after your set forever more—if you can find me."

"Let it wait," said Thane. "Start poking around the car insurance offices and some of the car dumps. I want to start a trace on any recent road smash write-offs. Who owned the car before the accident, what did they do with it afterwards—and particularly, who has the registration book."

The sergeant nodded. "Sammy Bell?"

"Maybe. Try it anyway."

As MacLeod left, Thane swung his gaze towards Phil Moss, still waiting patiently. "All we've really got is Sammy Bell. Right, Phil, you and I will concentrate on him. It's time we took a look at this filling station."

He lifted the desk phone, and waited impatiently until the station switchboard answered. "Joyce—I want the duty car at the front door in two minutes." Then, a penitent afterthought, he added. "And get me my wife on the phone, will you?"

"I'll get my hat." Moss rose from his chair, and headed for the door. "Say hello to Mary for me."

The pulsing buzz of the call went along the telephone line. Mary Thane didn't take long to answer. Policemen's wives seldom do.

"It's me, dear," he began apologetically. "Busy?"

"No—drinking coffee as usual." The soft chuckle took the sting from the words. Mary Thane had a sense of humour. When you were a cop's wife, it helped. "Any idea yet when you'll be home?"

"Can't tell, dear. We've landed a tough one."

Her voice became more concerned. "Colin, you're remembering what today is?"

"Tom? No, I haven't forgotten." There was a large parcel in one corner of his office, ready and waiting for his son's tenth birthday. "Look, unless something absolutely drastic happens, I'll make it home for six tonight—though I'll probably have to go back out later."

She relaxed. "Good. He was getting worried. The postman brought a small avalanche of presents this morning, but I'm keeping them till he gets back from school. Oh, and Colin, he wants you to invite Phil for tea."

Thane grinned. Detective Inspector Phil Moss might defend his bachelor status as keeping him free of family ties—but he was in considerable demand in the Thane household as an honorary uncle.

He said good-bye, replaced the receiver, and, whistling softly, pulled open the bottom drawer of his desk. Most of its space seemed covered by a tangle of socks, dirty handkerchiefs, and unsharpened pencils. He shoved one bundle aside, and lifted out a collection of small, soft-covered notebooks, each time-darkened cover held in place by an elastic band. Any cop with a grain of sense stored his used notebooks—and not merely as a future aid to some possible volume of memoirs. This bundle dated back to the time before he had been transferred to the Millside Division, and they still came in useful. He thumbed through the books, found the one he wanted, and flicked through its pages. At last he located the entry he'd been seeking, folded down one corner of the page to mark the place, put the book in his pocket, and went down to the waiting car.

It was a twenty-minute journey to the filling station, most of the route lying across city, the traffic flow becoming progressively busier as one by one lesser roads joined the main trunk route south. A first few drops of rain formed on the police car's windscreen; then, as the drizzle gained strength, the twin wipers began their monotonous sweep. At last, the Jaguar, indicator light flashing, turned out of the main stream, purred over a short concrete run-in, and stopped just short of the filling station pumps.

In layout, the place was a masterpiece of cost-saving functional simplicity. Behind the pumps, with their umbrella canopy, lay a single L-shaped block, a flat-roofed concrete structure, painted white. Its main face was two-thirds occupied by a tiny glass-fronted showroom, designed to hold two cars but at that moment only occupied by a new Renault saloon. A small office was located in the remaining section, and the entire building was dwarfed by the giant neon sign which sprouted from its roof.

"Looks ordinary enough," said Moss, peering through the Jaguar's rain-beaded passenger window. "Well, where do we start, Colin?"

"There's our man." Thane gestured towards the open doorway of the office. A white-overalled figure came hurrying out, wiping his hands on the inevitable rag as the two detectives left the car and began to walk towards him. Then the pump attendant stopped, frowning as he spotted the uniformed driver behind the Jaguar's steering wheel. Another car roared up the concrete run-in and stopped beside the pumps. The pump attendant hesitated, business instincts triumphing, and made a fast job of feeding five gallons into the new arrival's tank. The driver handed over cash, received his change from the leather bag slung over the pump man's shoulder, then drove off with a wave.

"Now, gents." The attendant, thin, middle-aged, and balding, turned towards them. "Police?"

Thane nodded.

"You'll be out about Sammy." His voice was solemn. "I wondered where he'd got to when he didn't show up for work. Then I found a story in the morning paper." He shook his head sadly. "These road accidents. You never know the minute your turn's coming." The drizzle of rain grew heavier. "Better come into the office," he suggested.

They followed him into the building. The office was a small ten-by-eight room, furnished with a small desk, a chair, a telephone, and a small radiator. The rest of the available space was taken up by a display board covered in chromium-plated car accessories, the floor around it sur-rounded by a small mountain of cartons and boxes.

"Side lines." The man thumbed towards the pile. "Inner tubes, wing mirrors, safety belts—you name it, we've got it." He sat on the chair, saddle-fashion. "I'm Len Field. What can I do for you?"

Thane carried out his side of the introductions. "How many of a staff do you have here?" he asked.

"There were just the pair of us," said the pump attendant. "The place was only opened about eight months ago, and it was me and another bloke who manned it for a spell. Then he had a row with the boss, and Sammy got his job. I looked after the cash side of things, and Sammy split the pump work with me and took care of the workshop—it's round the back."

"We're trying to find out where he was living," said Thane. "We located a brother—but he couldn't help."

The pump attendant nodded wisely. "Sammy told me he didn't get on with his family. He'd been a bit down on his luck, and they wouldn't lift a finger to help." It was a slightly twisted truth, but the late Sammy Bell had obvi-ously convinced his colleague that he was the victim of heartless circumstance. "Well, you don't have to look any further, Chief Inspector."

"He stayed here?"

The man gestured over his shoulder. "There's a wee store-room beside the workshop. Sammy fitted it out with a bed and a hot plate. Oh, it was all right," he hastily reassured them. "The boss knew all about it. Matter of fact, that's why all these boxes are lying around in here. Made us a bit short of space."

Phil Moss stirred from his position beside the glowing

heater. "Your boss must have had a pretty soft spot for him, eh?"

Len Field agreed. "Old Mr. Millan's pretty decent. His nephew's on his way over right now. Once I saw the piece about the accident in the paper, I phoned our head office. Young Erick said he'd take a trip out."

"Erick Millan?" Thane was no sporting fan, but for more than a year now it had been hard to find a Grand Prix report in any paper which did not have some reference to the latest performance notched by the still comparative newcomer to the big-time racing game. Millan's performances still lay short of greatness. But the world of speed tagged him a driver gradually edging his way into the aristocracy of the circuits.

The pump attendant gave an anxious glance through the filling station window. "I'll need to get out to the pumps. There's a car waiting." To emphasise his words, a motor horn gave an impatient blast. He took a key from the pegboard on the wall, and handed it to Thane. "If you want to check over Sammy's things, you can go round the back. We've only two keys to the storeroom. This one's mine—Sammy must have had the other one with him."

Pulling the rag from his pocket, he went out of the door, wiping his hands yet again as he headed through the rain towards the pumps. They followed him from the office, then turned left and skirted the side of the filling station. Behind the block, the workshop's double door lay open. They went in, glad to be once more sheltered from the drenching drizzle.

The workshop was small, little bigger than a domestic garage in size, yet beautifully equipped. Most of the floor space was occupied by a powerful-looking breakdown truck. A workbench ran along one complete wall of the building, an extravagant array of tools littered along its surface. A lathe was mounted in a central position, and a compressor pump, designed to feed the forecourt air-hose, occupied the faraway corner.

Moss gave a low whistle. "Take a look at the roof beams," he invited.

A full set of chain-pulleyed block and tackle lay waiting, supported by metal crossbeams. And there was other equipment, nearer ground level. Gas cylinders for an oxy-acetylene cutter-welder plant, a small pillar of new tyres, still in their factory wrappings, even some one-gallon drums, tightly sealed but labelled as containing primer and cellulose paint. Sammy Bell had had enough equipment in hand to practically build a car of his own from scratch—or to carry out any conversions necessary to disguise a stolen car so that the most devoted owner wouldn't have recognised it.

"Interesting," agreed Thane. "Very interesting. Still, it's too early to jump to conclusions, Phil. Let's find this store-room."

They squeezed round the rear of the breakdown truck, dodged under the stubby boom of its crane-derrick, and located the door they'd been seeking. The pump attendant's key turned smoothly in the lock, the door swung open, and together they peered into the windowless gloom within. Thane found a light switch inside the doorway, snapped it down, and a bare electric bulb flared to life.

Sammy Bell's quarters had been far from luxurious. But a man used to a prison cell would probably have found them not lacking in comfort. Most of the available wall-space was covered by full-colour pin-up pictures salvaged from a variety of magazines. In each case the photographer concerned had obviously become so fascinated by the model before him that he'd decided clothes were an unnecessary encumbrance which would only have hidden some of the fine-focus anatomical detail.

The room's furnishings were simple. A hospital-type cot,

covered in coarse grey army blankets, was the principal item. An old beer-crate acted as a bedside table, with a portable radio and an ash tray resting on its top. The hotplate ring was mounted on metal legs beyond the bed, and Sammy had fixed shelving beside it to hold a miscellany of cups, dishes, and tins. A big metal stores cupboard, more pin-ups decorating its exterior, had obviously been used as a wardrobe. The place was neat enough—they teach you that "inside" until it can become a habit.

"Well, let's get started." Thane got to work on the wardrobe, while Moss turned his attention to the crowded shelves. They searched swiftly and carefully, returning each item to its former position. As long as they had to preserve the illusion of merely checking on a traffic fatality, even a hit-and-run killing, there could be no surface evidence left of a search which might have had a deeper, more penetrating motive.

Thane drew a blank at the wardrobe. There was a suit, pockets empty, a freshly laundered set of white overalls, some clean shirts and underclothes. But nothing more personal than a small tin box containing two sets of cuff-links remained to recall the man whose clothing lay waiting.

Turning from the shelves, Phil Moss checked his wrist watch, took out his tube of stomach pills, and swallowed two in quick succession. Face puckering at the sour taste which remained, he shook his head. "I get an awfully funny feeling that someone's been here before us," he declared. "Heck, Colin, look at that for a start." He pointed to a cut-down one-gallon petrol can which did obvious duty as a wastebasket. "Empty. Take away the clothes and groceries, and the place is like a ruddy hotel room after the guest has checked out and the cleaning squad have finished."

Down on his knees now, peering under the bed, Thane grunted agreement. "Looks like we're too late. Still—here, let's see what's in this." He dragged out a cheap fibre suitcase, dumped it on top of the bed, and pressed the twin catches. They flew open, and he threw back the lid.

Sammy seemed to have used the case as a general storehouse. An unopened half-bottle of whisky, a broached carton of cigarettes and a tin of lighter fuel lay alongside a bundle of paperback Westerns. Thane picked up a scuffed leather billfold, put it in his pocket, then rummaged deeper into the case, pushing aside a half-used box of paper handkerchiefs and a grease-stained pack of playing cards, the latter tied loosely by string.

"If I knew what you were looking for, maybe I could help." The voice from the storeroom doorway jerked them round. The man was small and stockily built, and wore a heavy sheepskin jacket over a dark blue lounge suit.

Erick Millan gave the quizzical grin which a hundred newspaper and television cameramen had already captured for their mass audiences. Fresh-faced, clean-shaven, his dark curly hair just beginning to thin on top, Millan might have been specially cast from a mould designed to produce a boy hero of the racing world.

"The pump attendant told me you'd be round here." He came into the room, peeled off his string-backed driving gloves, and shook his head. "Hell of a thing to happen. Bell was a damn good mechanic."

"On your team, Mr. Millan?" asked Thane.

The racing driver pursed his lips. "Nearly. You're Chief Inspector Thane, right?"

Thane nodded. "This is Detective Inspector Moss." He paused, then went on convincingly. "You know the details. Bell was knocked down and killed by a hit-and-run driver. Probably some drunk. We came over to take a look over his stuff, get a line on his next of kin, the usual routine. We've traced a brother, but their relationship was pretty strained and there may be a wife or someone else around."

Millan nodded. "Nasty sort of job—still, I suppose some-one's got to do it. Bit of a loss to us, too. Good all-round mechanics are hard to find, Chief Inspector."

"He'd plenty of equipment to work with, anyway," said Moss. "You've got quite a little workshop here."

The other man seemed pleased. "You like it? My idea—though my uncle wasn't very keen at the start."

He pulled a long, slim cigarette case from an inside pocket and offered it round, then snapped the built-in lighter for each in turn. "I'm sales director with Ascension Garages. Old Ludd Millan, my uncle, runs the whole shoot-ing match of course. And when we began building a string of these filling stations round the fringe of the city, well, his idea was they should be purely petrol agencies. But I said no, we should put a small workshop in each, and catch some of the local breakdown and maintenance trade." He took another draw on his cigarette. "I planned the workshop layouts so that one man could tackle almost every mechanical job that was likely to come our way."

"Worth while?" Thane showed polite interest.

"More than pays its way," answered Millan enthusiasti-cally.

Phil Moss scratched his neck with one hand. "How did you feel about Bell using this place as his home?"

Millan shrugged. "My uncle gave him the go-ahead, and I didn't mind as long as the word didn't spread around. We were probably breaking half a dozen health and housing bylaws—but, well, he'd nowhere else to go."

Thane turned back to the suitcase, rummaged once more through its contents, then straightened up. "Well, that's about it," he declared. "I'll get someone along to collect this stuff, and give your man a receipt. We'll hold it until his relatives lodge a claim."

They followed him out into the workshop, squeezing in turn past the bulk of the breakdown truck. Millan stopped by the lathe, rested one hand on its polished switchcase, and appeared troubled. "Look, Chief Inspector, I'd better tell you. Bell had, well, he'd been in trouble a few times. We knew that when my uncle took him on. In fact, he'd just come out of jail when we hired him."

"We've got his record, Mr. Millan," said Thane slowly. "But thank you."

The racing driver dropped his cigarette on the concrete floor, and ground it underfoot. "Bell laid it on the line to my uncle. He wanted a chance. And, well, Old Ludd doesn't often go to church—he says fifty per cent of people who do are simply taking out a comprehensive insurance against the hereafter. But he's inclined towards the occasional good deed. He gave Bell this job, and told him he could use the storeroom . . . and Bell was a good worker."

"You said he was nearly on your racing team. What did that amount to?" queried Thane.

The younger man seemed more at ease again. "Well, he knew about the cars, of course. I've got half a dozen men at our main garage who spend more time on my racing machinery than they do working for the cash customers. Bell used to come along some evenings and lend a hand. The team's taken a while to build up, and some of the men travel with me round the circuits. . . . I've got one of the best pit crews in the business. Well, Chief Inspector, Bell was keen, and a damn good engine tuner. I'd promised I'd squeeze him on the strength the first chance we had." He drew on his driving gloves. "Time I was moving. I've got a meeting to attend back in the office."

He stopped again at the workshop entrance, turned up the high collar of his sheepskin jacket, and flashed his quizzical grin. "Incidentally, Chief Inspector, I suppose I shouldn't ask—but are the police getting anywhere in this stolen car panic that's going on?" Their obvious surprise amused him. "I've got a pal at Headquarters. He told me about it a couple of weeks back. In fact, I wouldn't have been surprised if someone had come out to check up on Sammy Bell." He shook his head. "They'd have been wasting their time, though."

Thane mumbled noncommittally. "They're still working on it."

Erick Millan gave them a cheerful half-salute, and strode off. The two policemen exchanged glances, then followed at a slower pace. They reached the front of the filling station just as a powerful exhaust snarled to life. The bellow died, then rose again as Millan's small red-and-blue Sprite runabout moved away from the forecourt area. It paused at the road's edge, then darted off into the traffic.

The pump attendant came towards them. "Nice bloke, Mr. Erick. Well, gents, got all you wanted?"

"Just one or two more questions to ask you," said Thane. But his eyes were following the red-and-blue sports car, now disappearing into the distance.

CHAPTER TWO

Chief Detective Inspector Colin Thane was assembling a timetable—a timetable which covered the basic pattern of the life of the late Sammy Bell, now a silent husk in the red brick City Mortuary.

Len Field tried hard to oblige with answers, but there were gaps, long hours when the Ascension pump attendant could offer only hazy guesswork.

Still, the timetable began to form. The filling station, it seemed, normally operated from eight in the morning until ten at night, the two men working a loosely arranged shift system and Sammy Bell occasionally turning out through the night to answer after-hours distress calls from stranded motorists. In the ordinary day, Len Field took from eight A.M. until about noon, then went off until about six in the evening, remaining on duty from then until the pumps closed. He preferred it that way. The mornings were usually quiet, and the evening was the time when motorists were more likely to tell him to keep the change. Sammy Bell, on the other hand, had spent most mornings in the workshop unless he had time due him to compensate for an overnight call. He'd manned the filling station on his own during the afternoon, and stopped work about seven in the evening.

"Up till a month ago there was a girl with us during the day," sniffed Field. "Nose-in-the-air bit of stuff. Then it

turned out she was offering some of the customers more
than petrol. Somebody's wife complained to head office,
and she had to go."

"Bad for business." Thane was sympathetic.

"Very bad," agreed the pump man. "Sales were down
for weeks afterwards. Know what her name was, sir?
Prudence. Never can tell, can you?"

Moss turned a splutter into a cough, and turned away
to look at the Renault in the forecourt showroom.

"How about yesterday, now?" queried Thane. "Did you
and Bell keep to the usual routine?"

"Same as usual, sir. Sammy was called out to a breakdown in the morning—nothing much, though. A woman
with a flat battery."

Thane ignored the whimsical picture Field's words made
possible. "And at night?"

The pump man shrugged. "Same as usual again. Sammy
left just after seven. Said he was going to get some food,
and then he was going to meet someone."

"Man or woman?"

Field shook his head. "Didn't say. Sammy kept pretty
quiet about what you might call personal things. But I
don't think he had a girl, if that's what you mean. Never
saw any pals come around looking for him."

"Phone calls?"

"Once or twice," agreed the other man. "Somebody
called . . . Jacko, I think it was. But I don't know anything more than that, and I don't think he called yesterday."

There was nothing more to be gained from the pump
attendant. They said good-bye, and as the two detectives
returned to their car Len Field gave his hands a specially
thorough wipe on the rag and turned back towards his
pumps.

The rain clouds were clearing, and the drizzle had almost died, leaving the roads black and wet-sheened. The tyres hissed above the purring engine as the police car swung away from the filling station.

"Headquarters, driver," said Thane, settling back in his seat. "You'll have time to grab a quick meal in the canteen while we're there."

The uniformed man nodded his thanks. He was on a six-till-three shift, and was beginning to feel decidedly empty. His foot pressed a fraction more heavily on the accelerator.

The radio receiver crackled to life. It was a message for one of the Northern Division cars, busy in a chase after a smash-and-grab raider.

"They're welcome to it," sighed Moss, munching a tea biscuit from his emergency supply. Keep your stomach acids occupied, that was one of his golden rules in the ulcer battle. "Well, what do you make of things so far, Colin?"

Thane wrinkled his nose in disgust. "Watch where your crumbs are going," he grumbled, wiping some biscuit fragments from the side of his coat. "Right now, I want to know more about Erick Millan, and I'd like to know who Jacko is. Phil, that's two jobs for you when we get to Headquarters. Ask Modus Operandi if they've got a line on any ned nicknamed Jacko who may have teamed up with Sammy at some time. Then get hold of Jock Mills at the *Bugle* office. Tell him we want anything on Erick Millan he can dig out from their cuttings library."

There was no trouble in that. Jock Mills made a habit of co-operating with the Millside team, and keeping any resultant story in deep-freeze until he got the all clear. Quite a few by-line exclusives which had appeared in the *Bugle* owed their origin to the reporter's tacit acceptance of the unspoken rules.

"And Sammy Bell's gear?"

"We'll dump that one in the lap of the Scientific boys," said Thane. "But I'll give long odds they'll find nothing." He remembered the leather billfold he'd found in Bell's suitcase, took it from his pocket, and tossed it on to his companion's lap. "Empty. Probably a spare. No letter, no papers—you're right, Phil, someone was there before us. They didn't break in either. Remember the keys found in Bell's pockets? Whoever killed him played it very smartly. They kept him in storage somewhere while they took his keys, went to the filling station and searched around, then came back, put the keys back in his pocket, and took him out to that roadway."

Moss pondered the point. "What were they after, eh?"

They winced as a cyclist suddenly wobbled out from a side street into the path of the Jaguar. The uniformed driver swore, swung the wheel, then straightened the car on to its original path. Behind them, the cyclist pedalled happily onward.

"Probably they didn't know themselves—accepting there was more than one man involved," said Thane. "Maybe they just wanted to make sure he'd left nothing lying around which would point a finger at them. We still don't know whether they had him spotted as a potential 'grass' or simply decided that he was becoming a nuisance to have around the place, wanting more money than he was worth."

It was a point which worried Thane. If the car gang had labelled Sammy Bell as about to squeal, that could mean that the C.I.D. ghost squad man had also been marked. Yet he knew Headquarters would be reluctant to withdraw their undercover man unless there was direct evidence that his usefulness in the role was finished, and that his future had grown correspondingly dangerous. It took a long time, sometimes many months, to build up the kind of convincing front which allowed a "ghost" to slouch around the underworld, his presence ignored if not in fact accepted.

He forced his thoughts away from that nameless cop.
"You know, Phil, if they were using the filling station as a
wayside stop for hot cars it was a cosy setup. Once they
got a car there and inside the workshop, they could work
on it right through the night. All the equipment was handy.
It could be altered around, and even be a different colour
by morning."

Phil Moss put the last piece of biscuit in his mouth, and
gave a quiet belch. "How about Field?"

"The pump man?" Thane shook his head. "I think he's
on the up-and-up. According to him, every now and again
Sammy wasn't around in the morning. How many of these
overnight calls were genuine? And how many of these
mornings was he out looking for the next car. Run a check
on Field if you want—though I've a feeling all he knows
about cars is which end you pour in the petrol. I'm more
interested in Erick Millan."

"But Millan's a big name," protested Moss. "He's set up
to be a national hero before long—and he didn't give Bell
the job. That was his uncle's idea, and Ascension Garages
have a reputation that reads like an archbishop's character
reference."

The Headquarters building was its usual bustling self—
and a little more. The Rotary visitors, about thirty strong,
were still on the prowl under the shepherding care of a
perspiring uniformed inspector. They flooded down the
main stairway, flowed round Thane and Moss as the two
men entered the building, then disappeared into the Traffic
Department—a dutiful, gossiping mass of solid citizenry.

"See you later, then." Leaving Moss to get to a telephone
and begin his chores, Thane took the elevator up to the
second floor, turned left along the corridor there, and entered the jealously guarded precincts of the Scientific
Branch. Dan Laurence was in his room, a small, tobacco-

stale office furnished in spartan style, and as Thane entered he got up, swept a pile of reports, books, and old newspapers from the only spare chair and made him welcome.

"You're a wee bit earlier than I expected," apologised the superintendent, lowering his portly form chairwards again. "Still, we should have things about ready. And Doc Williams should be over in a few minutes. He said he'd come straight across from the mortuary as soon as they got finished with the post-mortem." He flicked the intercom switch on his desk and gave a bellow which showed a complete lack of faith in the mechanics of the relay. "Willie —are you there?"

"Sir." The detective on the other end acted with a speed generated from bitter past experience.

"Get off your backside and bring through all we've got on the Bell job." The Scientific Branch boss released the switch, and directed a friendly glare towards Thane. "How's the leg work going, Colin?"

"Slow, but becoming interesting," said Thane cautiously. "Bell lived in a room behind one of the Ascension filling stations. I'd like your squad to look it over, Dan. But we'll have to do it quietly—Buddha's orders are we still play this as a hit-and-run accident."

"I follow—but what are we after?" frowned Laurence.

"Somebody beat us to it and had a general clean-up before we arrived," explained Thane. "But there might be something lying around. It's pretty vague, I know—anyway, the pump attendant's expecting us back. I told him we'd collect Bell's gear, and hold it for relatives. Now if a couple of your men could go out with the van . . ."

Laurence finished it for him. "They could give the room a going-over while they were at it, and nobody any the wiser. Prints, maybe?"

With a smart tap on the office door, one of Laurence's

team entered the room. Wearing a hospital-style white coat, he looked more like a first-year medical student than a detective constable.

"Just finished, sir." He handed over two close-typed report sheets.

"Good." Laurence pondered. "Started that spectro analysis for Argyll County yet?"

"Getting it set up now, Super," said his junior.

"Leave it. Get hold of Tommy and lay on a van. I've a wee bit of work here that calls for a cautious, intelligent approach, but we'll just need to make do with you two. Come back in fifteen minutes, and I'll give you the details."

The youngster grinned and left. Laurence settled down to reading the report sheets, taking his time, apparently oblivious of Thane's impatient presence. At last, with a sigh, he turned his attention back to their visitor.

"Sorry, Colin. There's little you don't know already. Traces of motor oil on the clothes, a few specks of cellulose here and there. Sort of thing you'd expect from a man working around a garage. Tyre tread patterns—you had that before. Metal filings among dust from trouser turn-ups." He pursed his lips in disappointment, and glanced down at the sheets again, continuing his summary. "This might be helpful if you ever get to court. His shoes were comparatively dry, and the soles had traces of grit from a concrete floor. The way my boys see it, he didn't walk to South Salisbury Road. If what Doc said earlier was right, this ties in. Sammy Bell was taken there by car, direct from somewhere with a concrete floor, then dumped."

The telephone shrilled a long peal. Laurence picked up the receiver.

"Aye, he's here," he told the caller. "Hold on." He handed the phone across to Thane. "Doc Williams, wanting you."

The police surgeon was apologetic as his voice came over

the line. "Sorry I can't make it, Thane. There's been a bit of trouble over in the Southern Division. Couple of uniformed men need patching, but I thought you'd like to know the p.m. results before I go."

"I need all the facts I can get," agreed Thane. "What's the verdict?"

"As before. He was lying on the ground when he was run over—and the patrolman was right. The car reversed back across him again. Injuries and bruising leave no doubt on that score. Still, he was almost definitely unconscious before it happened. We found signs of a blow on the head administered some time before death."

"Anything else?"

Doc Williams spoke quickly and quietly to someone else at his end of the line. Then he replied, "Well, he had a meal about an hour before. And there was a small third-degree burn on the thumb and first finger of his right hand, with some charring of skin tissue. I'd say he grabbed hold of a live electric wire. Nothing serious, Thane. Sort of thing a mechanic might get if he was working around a car and didn't disconnect the battery." The usual cautious qualification followed his words. "Mind you, that's only a guess."

"Thanks, Doc. It may help." Thane scribbled a brief note on the scratch-pad pushed towards him. "You'll let me have it in full later?"

"Soon as I get organised and can put my secretary to work," promised the police surgeon.

Thane replaced the phone, and rose. "Time I was moving," he told Laurence.

"Could Doc help any?"

"At this stage, who knows?" shrugged Thane. "We're gathering up the pieces, but what I need is someone to tell me how to put them together. Any idea who was working with Doc on the p.m.?"

"MacMaster, I think." Laurence wrinkled his nose. "If the old buzzard got wind of it you'd have had to tie him down to keep him away."

Professor MacMaster, university lecturer in forensic medicine, a thin, gloomy figure who cast a corpse-like shadow all his own, had an almost magical habit of being on hand when an interesting piece of dissection work came along. His only other interest was stamp-collecting. If MacMaster had been with Doc, then their combined conclusions would form a cast-iron reconstruction of the death of the corpse concerned.

He thanked Laurence again, then headed back down to the ground floor. Phil Moss was in the inspectors' room at the canteen—white linen table covers and waitress service for the senior staff instead of the plastic tops and cafeteria-style layout of the main area. There were a few other officers in the room, who nodded a greeting as Thane weaved between the tables to where his somewhat reluctant Detective Inspector was now hastily finishing a plateful of steamed fish.

"Give me another couple of minutes," pleaded Moss, forking busily.

Thane pulled out the chair next to his second in command, ordered tea and a sandwich from the waitress who had appeared almost at his elbow, then brought Phil up to date. His order arrived as he finished the summary.

"How about your end of it?" he demanded, taking a first bite at the sandwich.

Fish finished, Moss lit a cigarette. "Jock Mills is sending on all the cuttings he can find on Erick Millan. I asked him to add in any he had on Millan's uncle or Ascension Garages while he was at it." He took another drag at the cigarette and, ignoring a scowl from a passing white-aproned Amazon, flicked the ash into his saucer. "Jock had some time on his hands, and I got him to read me some of

Erick Millan's background over the phone. Racing drivers come under the 'bad risk' category as far as the newspaper world's concerned. They keep an up-to-date obituary handy on them just in case they get written off in a crash."

Thane mumbled through his sandwich. "Let's have it."

"Right." Moss leaned back on the wooden-framed chair. "Young Millan's twenty-five and a bachelor. He plays the field as far as women are concerned, and between his looks and his profession he doesn't have to work very hard on them. Father was an army officer, killed in action with the Armoured Corps at El Alamein. Mother died a few years back, and his uncle's the only relative left. Uncle isn't married, and Erick is his blue-eyed boy. So when uncle pops off, Erick gets Ascension Garages—unless he kills himself first." He paused, watched Thane take another large bite of sandwich. "That meat's more fat than lean—bad for the heart. Anyway, Millan has been racing for about four seasons now. The first couple of years he was playing about in small club events, but finally he hit a winning streak, good enough for one of the big works teams to look him over and give him a tryout. Then he signed on with that private Ferrari team. Remember last year's Le Mans?"

"Vaguely." The sports pages, apart from boxing, were relatively unknown territory to Thane. "He did pretty well there, didn't he?"

"Pretty well?" Moss snorted. "He was lying third—then the co-driver took over and crashed the thing fifth time round. But Millan isn't the type who fits into a team. He's too fond of his own way—the complete individualist. So there was a bit of a burst-up, and now he's back racing his own cars. The motoring writers think he's the brightest British prospect in years."

Thane took a last swallow of tea and rose, still chewing. "We'll see a lot more of Mr. Millan before we're finished," he prophesied. "Come on, time we were moving."

Puzzled, Phil Moss fell into step as they left the canteen and headed out into the Headquarters yard where their car and driver waited, both refuelled.

"Where now?" he demanded.

"If we're going to be so tangled up in the stolen car racket, we might as well get some expert advice," said Thane, a surprising twinkle in his eyes. "Someone you've never met, Phil." He patted his left-hand pocket, feeling the notebook beneath the cloth. "You'll find it . . . interesting."

This time the police Jaguar headed due north, leaving the tall buildings behind, penetrating into the new housing suburbs on the city's outskirts, purring past rows of identically fronted bungalows and semi-villas, each with its sprouting television aerial, its minute, hedge-guarded patch of well-tended garden. Thane peered anxiously ahead. It was a few years since he'd been out this way, and in that short time building development had changed the entire contour of the land around. A busy, brand-new shopping centre squatted its concrete bulk where he remembered an old farm house, fringed with trees. Then he spotted one landmark which hadn't changed, the spire of a small, red stone church.

"Next on the right." The uniformed driver swung the wheel, and the car turned off the main highway and up a narrow side road. A short distance along, Thane signalled him to stop, and the car halted beside a compact villa-style house built from the same local red stone as the church they'd passed, and obviously considerably older than the cement-wash and pebble-dash bungalows which faced it across the road. The house had a wide stretch of garden, laid out in grass except for a tiny rather overgrown rose patch in its centre. A broad tarmacadam driveway led from the pavement's edge, skirted the grass and the front of the house, and led round the faraway corner.

"We've arrived." Thane was amused at his companion's growing bewilderment. They left the driver on radio watch, and walked along the driveway, passed the house, and turned the corner.

Phil Moss gave a grunt of surprise. Set back from the house, hidden till that moment, was a large brick and corrugated-iron structure, neatly painted cream but remaining in both style and shape something close to an architectural nightmare.

MURDOCK MOTORS said the small, green-lettered sign fastened just above eye level on the wall facing them. Farther back, the driveway widened into a respectable-sized parking lot, currently occupied by an old single-deck motor bus and a pair of close-parked, dust-covered saloon cars of doubtful vintage.

Sure of his way now, Thane marched across the tarmac and led Moss to the rear of the building. A pair of big double doors lay open, and they walked into the gloom of the workshop beyond. Moss looked around, then pointed towards a big blue Austin saloon. A pair of dungaree-clad legs projected from beneath, the feet encased in light canvas shoes which wriggled as their owner exerted pressure on some unseen mechanical problem.

Metal sounded on metal, then the tool slipped and jangled down on to concrete. A hiss of exasperation came from beneath the car, and a hand groped blindly.

"Who are we looking for?" asked Moss. "Murdock?"

Thane nodded.

Phil Moss went over and gave a sharp rap on the car's bonnet. "Hey—come out a minute, will you?"

A growl of metal wheels on concrete sent him jumping back as the worker below shot out from beneath the car, propelling the mobile platform he'd been lying on with one short, powerful leg-movement.

The man was small, fat, and about fifty. His bald head gleamed with perspiration except where a broad black oil-stain streaked a zigzag path. Still lying on his back, he raised an inquiring eyebrow. "Didn't hear you come in, chum. . . ." Then his voice died away as he looked beyond Moss, and his face crinkled into a beam of welcome. "Mr. Thane! Well, what brings you here—give us a hand up, mate." He grasped Moss's extended hand and struggled to his feet, moving his shoulders with a sigh of relief. "Man could die of cramp under there."

Solemnly, but with considerable warmth, Ben Murdock shook hands with Thane and gave a friendly nod as Phil Moss was introduced.

"Things haven't changed much." Thane glanced round the garage workshop. "How's business? Still running the place on your own?"

Ben Murdock patted the Austin's wing with one grease-stained hand. "This one's got to be back on the road by tonight. One o' the lads is off sick, and the other one's out wi' the jeep on a breakdown. Just thought I might as well get on wi' the job myself."

"Round about here should be a good area for business," said Moss, in an attempt to cement friendly relations.

"Good enough," agreed Murdock. But his face darkened. "Don't thank the local council for that, though. They tried to heave me out—ruddy bilge 'bout town 'n country planning and me spoiling the look of the place. But I told 'em a thing or two—such as what I thought of those mass-produced living-boxes they were putting up all around." He chuckled. "Then we had a wee compromise, like. No more talk o' putting me off my ground, and I wouldn't sell out to a man who wanted to build a bingo hall."

"A bingo hall?"

"Heck, he didn't exist," admitted Murdock. "But you've never seen a council shut up so quickly." He paused, his light blue eyes narrowing shrewdly. "You didn't come out here, either o' you, to ask after my business. What's up, Mr. Thane?"

Thane leaned against the side of the car, tracing a pattern on its polished paintwork. "We've got a spot of bother on our plate, Ben. I thought you could maybe help."

Murdock digested the information, swaying a little on the flat heels of his canvas shoes. "The old game, eh. Well . . . can't say no, can I? Come on over to the house—Ida's there."

The two detectives in his wake, Murdock padded from the workshop, out across the yard, and headed for the rear door of the villa. He waved them in, and they squeezed past into a bright-tiled kitchen, its walls lined with a spotless array of white and cream household units. A coffee percolator bubbled noisily on a small table in one corner, two cups waiting ready beside it.

"Is that you, Ben?" The woman's voice came faintly through the half-opened inner door. Then she appeared in the entrance, and gave a surprised gurgle of delight.

Ida Murdock was small and on the same plump lines as her brother. In her early forties, her generous figure encased in tight slacks and a heavy fisherman knit red sweater, her greying hair in an unexpected urchin cut, she bustled into the room, her arms outstretched. "Mr. Thane—it's nice to see you. It's been years . . ."

Thane grabbed her hands to forestall the threatened embrace. "You're looking well, Miss Murdock," he told her, aware of the grin spreading on Moss's face as the other man saw his obvious embarrassment.

She giggled. "Still full of compliments."

Deciding it was safe, Thane released his grip. The woman

looked him up and down. "You've put on some weight," she said in a slightly critical tone.

"I'm a Chief Inspector now," he grimaced. "When you're a Chief Inspector you're allowed to get fat—looks more respectable."

"Hmmph." She glanced towards Moss. "Is he one of yours?"

"Phil, come and be introduced." Thane beckoned him over. "Miss Ida Murdock, Detective Inspector Moss."

Miss Murdock shook hands with considerable energy. "Any friend of Mr. Thane's is welcome here," she assured him. With sudden caution and a birdlike dart of her head, she turned to Thane again. "It—it is just a friendly call, isn't it?"

He reassured her. "Purely friendly—I'm looking for help, and Ben's the only one I know who might be able to give it."

She relaxed again, took two more cups and saucers from the sideboard. "We'll have some coffee first. How do you like it?"

"Black—and three spoonfuls," replied Thane as she waved them to chairs round the table.

"Same for you, Mr. Moss?"

Phil Moss looked at the treacle-black brew and gave a near shudder. "Very white—no sugar."

"Hmm." She looked him up and down. "You know, you don't look overstrong for a policeman. You need building up a bit."

"Blame his bachelor existence," advised Thane, with a malicious grin. "He needs somebody like you to look after him."

Ida Murdock giggled again, then poured the coffee. Phil Moss shrank further back into his corner seat, very much aware of the increased interest in the light blue eyes as his cup was passed across.

"Mr. Thane . . ." Ben Murdock hesitated. "Your Inspector knows about me?"

Thane shook his head. "Not yet."

Murdock chewed on his lip for a moment. "Well, it's like this, Mr. Moss. Eight years past and more I got into a bit o' a scrape. Ida an' me run the business here—and there was a spell when I was a mug, a real gold-plated mug. Got in tow with some of the fellows who don't worry too much about whose money they're spending. Ever heard o' the stocking plan?"

Moss waited, interested.

"Some o' the hire-purchase firms run it. Och, it's straight enough—lets a dealer who hasn't much cash to play wi' build up a stock of motors for his showroom. They lend him the money, then as soon as he sells the car, he pays it back an' so on. Well," he sighed, "we sell a motor or two here, but we'd never done more than that. Then this sleek-haired bloke I'd seen aroun' the sales—said he was an ex-major—says would I like to come in wi' him in a new firm. Needed my experience, he said—there'd be so much cash down from each of us, then the stocking plan, and we'd have a nice wee showroom in the town . . . he'd got an inside tip about a firm that was packing in."

The mere retelling obviously angered his sister. "He took us in all right, Mr. Moss . . . fancy plans and a voice like the minister down the road."

"All right, Ida, I'm tellin' it." Her brother stopped her, his gruff voice surprisingly firm. "Well, we start off like that, see, and begin sellin' cars. Only I wasn't there much o' the time, what with keeping the garage here going. What Ida 'n I didn't know was that this bloke wasn't just not payin' back the stocking-plan money, but was working a fiddle when he sold the motors too. He'd fix up hire-purchase for a customer, see—at least that's the way it looked on the forms. Except sometimes the man who 'bought' the car might be a pal o' his an' the down payment was something which just happened on paper, usin' any old name and address an' the pal getting a tenner for the trouble. So this partner of mine gets a fat load of cash from the h.p. men for some old banger. He's still got the stocking-plan advance, which he doesn't bother about repaying—an' all the second h.p. firm can do when the pal doesn't pay the instalments is try and get the car back."

Moss gave a low whistle. It was a get-rich-quick plan with only one inevitable ending. "One day everything caught up with you."

The garage man nodded. "The stocking-plan firm found out, and repossessed their cars. Some o' them that were genuine sales, maybe for cash, were taken back from customers who didn't know a thing that had been happening. You see, legal like, the cars never really belonged to us at all. The customers started sueing us for their money back—and then the ordinary h.p. firm moved in too an' began making more trouble."

Still trying to grapple with the intricacies of the deals presented to him, conscious of strained effort behind Murdock's emotionless tones, Moss guessed the next stage. "That's when the police came in."

"Aye, an' lucky for me it was Mr. Thane here, who'd just new been made an inspector then." Murdock's eyes blazed. "But you know why the police came in? This bloke wasn't content wi' just fiddling the h.p. He'd been workin' another flanker . . . some of the cars we had, stuff he'd bought in secondhand under the stocking plan, were stolen ones . . . doctored up a bit, an' fitted up with registration books frae insurance write-offs. I could have been put away for years. . . ."

Thane held up his hand in protest. "Look, Ben, you

were simply the victim in it all—just as much as some of
the poor devils who bought the cars."

Ben Murdock shrugged. "Maybe. But you sorted the
whole stinkin' mess out. I could have been in the jail wi'
that other bloke, and I know it." He leaned forward, elbows
on the table. "Anyway, that's what happened. Now, what
is it you want, eh?"

Thane drew out the little black notebook, flicked over
the pages of long-ago cases, and found the entry he wanted.
"We're after another car gang, Ben. A bigger one. You've
been in the trade a long time, and you know most people
in it. What's happened to the men who were mixed up in
your own case—not just the ones who were sent away, but
the others we knew were working on the fringes? I've got
some names here from that time—just names of men with
no convictions, which means they've no record and we
don't know what they're doing or where they are." It was
a long, blind shot he was taking, one backed only by the
Modus Operandi department's staunch declaration that
once a man starts in crime he usually keeps to one branch
of it and one only. "How about . . ." he selected a name
at random from the eight-year-old list. "How about Drongo
Thetford?"

Murdock shook his head. "Out of it. Died from t.b. two
years back."

"Rick Martin?"

"Nope. He's married and workin' for a bookie."

The rest of the list was dealt with, one by one. When
it was finished, only two names remained.

"Big John Carner. You say he's still somewhere in the
trade. And Eddie Sloy—no trace." Thane put a pencilled
cross beside the two names. "Ben, can you find out for me?"

The garageman nodded. "Give me till tomorrow."

Ida came with them to the door, and waved energetically
as the police car drove away. Thane returned the wave

with a grin—but Phil Moss could raise only a rather weak smile.

"That woman," he growled. "You can come out on your own next time."

It was three o'clock in the afternoon and, amid the bustle of the city centre, Puggy Carson was on business bent. The casual onlooker might have been deceived on this count, for Puggy, in a quiet grey suit, well-polished brown shoes, and a dark green knitted silk tie, bore all the outward appearance of being in no hurry to get anywhere. A second glance at his untidy walk, faint built-in swagger, and rather crumpled facial contours would probably have resulted in the verdict that here was that rare animal, a successful punter. One who might at some time in the past have had frequent and rather painful acquaintance with the business end of a boxing glove.

Puggy turned out of busy Renfield Street into the comparative quiet of West George Street where a long line of cars, parked nose in to the pavement on the north side, stretched far into the distance like the split backbone of some gigantic herring. After the morning's rain, the sun had come out again, soaking up the moisture. A few of the hardier or more determined young women tripping past were wearing summer frocks and, he decided, life was reasonably pleasant.

"Should find one here," he murmured, strolling along and recalling the day's orders while he ran an expert eye over the waiting cars.

To Puggy, a car park was something similar to a gigantic self-service motor showroom—except that there was no bill to pay when you drove away. The entire tools of his trade were stored in the inside pocket of his jacket . . . two small pieces of brazing wire, each with a hook bend on one end; a heavy rubber sucker with small handle attached; a "jumper" made up from a short length of insulated wire with a bulldog clip fore and aft, a three-inch strip of narrow aluminium foil, and, a purely personal affair, his stop watch.

Near the junction with Wellington Street he made his choice. The Ford, in gleaming two-tone paintwork, was obviously in immaculate condition, bodywork unscarred and its registration number showing it to be one of the newer disc-brake models.

It would fill the bill. Puggy glanced around, ignoring the occasional passer-by but satisfying himself that there were no police uniforms in sight. One hand went into his pocket to press the stop-watch button, and then he got down to work.

First, the brazing wires. Standing close to the driver's side, he took out the two lengths and used one quick, experienced wrist movement to feed them through between the rubber sealing strips at the side of the quarter-light flap. A pull on one hook, located against the locking button on the window snib, pressed the button into the release position. An almost simultaneous twist on the second hook, gripping round the snib itself, moved it free. He brought the wires back out, pushed open the triangular glass, reached through and unlocked the door.

Eight seconds . . .

Puggy opened the driver's door, reached below the instrument panel, and pulled the bonnet release. He walked round to the front of the car, raised the bonnet, spared a theatrical moment to look at the engine, purse his lips, and shake his head.

Fourteen seconds . . .

The bulldog wire was next. One clip on to the positive terminal of the battery, the other to the low tension terminal on the coil. The tiny length of aluminium foil next, sliding smoothly into place to bridge the solenoid terminals

on the other side of the engine block. He pressed the rubber
solenoid button, listened to the sweet, swift grind of the
starter, then the engine fired.

Thirty-one seconds . . .

He shut the bonnet, walked round, got into the Ford,
released the handbrake, and backed the car out of the
parking line.

Puggy engaged first gear, fumbled for his stop watch,
and pressed the arrestor button. He drove off leisurely,
quietly, and waited until he had turned off and reached
Sauchiehall Street before he took out the watch.

Forty-eight seconds. He gave a chuckle of satisfaction.
Eight seconds less than the last time, though he could
hardly be blamed for the fact that the previous car of that
make he had tackled had obviously been in need of some
carburettor adjustment.

There was no reason for hurry now, and little for worry.
Puggy reckoned on pretty long odds against a driver's returning to his car within half an hour. If it did happen,
well, there were a few minutes of grace after that before the
police were contacted and a general description was broad-
cast. Getting the car started was the danger period—after
that you could relax, especially when journey's end was a
comparatively short distance away.

Still, he glanced in the rear mirror just to make sure,
turned off Sauchiehall Street before the Charing Cross
Junction where there was normally at least one standby
pointsman on duty, and threaded a zigzag course through
half a dozen side streets before turning into Peaceview
Terrace, two gaunt rows of grey four-storey tenements.
Slowing, dropping into bottom gear, he turned the car off
the road and into a narrow arched-over entry. The lane
beyond ran for about thirty feet to the entrance to a large
wooden hut, its dilapidated tin roof and faded paintwork

in tune with the battered sign MENRAN AUTO ELECTRICS above the opened double doors.

Puggy drove the car in, heard the double doors shut behind him, and treated himself to the luxury of a muscle-satisfying stretch.

"Switch the ruddy engine off," grumbled the man who'd closed the doors. "Never heard of carbon monoxide?"

"Okay, Jacko." It would have taken much more than that to ruffle Puggy Carson in his present sense of well-being. He got out, raised the car bonnet, and released the bulldog clip from the battery terminal. The engine died away, and he pulled out his cigarettes. "Smoke?"

"Ta." Mournfully, Jacko Menran waited for a light, then let the first lungful of smoke trickle from his long nose. "Any trouble?"

"Never is. Here . . ." Puggy brandished the stop watch with obvious pride. "What do you think of that, eh? Forty-eight seconds."

"Not bad." The stop-watch routine was beginning to prey on Jacko's nerves. Puggy's moods seemed almost ruled by the success or failure represented by its timings. "You've to phone in."

"Okay, okay." Puggy shrugged aside the reminder. "It can wait a minute." He brought out a small notebook and pencil, licked the lead, then carefully noted the timing. Behind him, Jacko was already at work stripping off the Ford's registration plates and substituting a fresh set from a waiting brown paper parcel.

"Got the registration book?"

"Over on the bench." Jacko finished fixing the new front plate, and stood back to admire his handiwork. "You'd better make that call."

"Uh-huh." Puggy moved towards the phone. "Pity about Sammy Bell, wasn't it?"

Jacko spat a loose flake of tobacco from his tongue and picked up the second plate. "I should weep."

"Callous basket, aren't you?" Puggy lifted the phone and began to dial.

Old Ludd Millan grumbled to himself, took off his reading glasses, and frowned across the desk at his nephew. Tall, with heavy, bushy eyebrows and close-cropped grey hair, he was a formidable figure. "Did you pass this stores estimate?" he demanded, gesturing towards the single sheet of paper on the otherwise bare surface of his desk. "A clear desk means a tidy mind"—that was Old Ludd's motto.

"Yes, why? Anything wrong?" Erick Millan stood before him, expression bland and friendly, but anticipating what was to come.

"Too damned high," scowled his uncle. "You could have trimmed at least two suppliers down a bit, Erick. You should know better. And that's not all. What's gone wrong with our car sales figures for the past two weeks? The turnover's dropped by over three thousand pounds."

Erick Millan scratched one ear. "Demand's fallen off a bit, Uncle. Nothing I can do about it." He contemplated a spot six inches above the older man's head. "You cut back the last advertising schedule, remember? How can I move cars if I can't let people know what we've got on offer?"

"Huh." Old Ludd pondered the point. "Sit down, Erick."

Millan raised an eyebrow, but dragged over the spare chair.

"How did you get on when you went out to see about Bell's effects?" Old Ludd pursed his lips. "Nasty business, Erick—tragic. I've been looking up the files, trying to trace any relatives."

His nephew was suitably sober. "The police were at the filling station when I got there. Two C.I.D. men, called Thane and Moss. They're taking charge of his things until they sort out the next-of-kin question. According to Field, the pump man, they've traced a brother or someone like that."

The older man contemplated the tips of his fingers, blunt, still with the faint scars of earlier years of knuckle-barking, skin-tearing spanner work. "I phoned the police after you went out, of course. Told them about him working for us . . . though they'd discovered that by then. The man I spoke to—in the Traffic section—said all they know is that it was probably some medium-sized saloon that hit him. They can tell that from the tyre marks, but there's little else they can establish."

"Probably some drunk—usually is when it's a hit-and-run accident." There was scant concern in the racing driver's tone. "Pity about Bell, though—losing him, I mean, apart from anything else. He was a first-class mechanic, despite his record."

His uncle glanced up, nostrils flaring slightly. "Don't judge a man by his past, Erick. What matters is his present and future, I've told you before. That's why I gave Bell a chance when he came to me."

"Good mechanics are scarce, too," murmured Millan.

Old Ludd ignored the aside. "I told the police to contact us if—ah—there was any difficulty regarding funeral expenses, that sort of thing. And we'll need to find another man for the filling station. Field can't run that place on his own."

His nephew brightened. "Want me to take care of that?"

"No. We'll advertise, then interview." The older man got up, towering a good six inches above the head of his nephew. He strode over to the window of the room, then turned. "Erick, I'm not happy about these sales figures—in fact, I'm not very happy with your work at all just now. You've got to keep at it, boy. For a start, let's try a fresh approach to the used-car side. I'd like you to spend the week end analysing the whole position, including the advertising, and come up with some good hard selling ideas by Monday."

"But . . ." Millan hesitated. "Sorry, it can't be done. This is Thursday. I'm going off tomorrow night. We're racing at Charterhall on Sunday, remember?"

Old Ludd smacked one fist down on the windowsill in sudden anger. "Blast it, Erick, racing may be important to you. But this is business, and business should come first. That's where too much of your time is going—on these cars. No business, no racing . . . remember that."

Millan's temper flared in turn. "Not the way I see it. Don't kid yourself that what you give me runs the team." He sneered. "It hardly covers the mechanics' time, and you damn well know it."

Old Ludd flushed. "What about the workshop facilities, eh? And where does the rest of the money come from anyway, Erick? Tell me, because I don't know. How about the two new engine blocks that arrived last week? Specially machined jobs, high alloy castings; you can't concentrate on that kind of power plant development without spending, really spending."

"They're not charged to the firm, if that's your worry," the racing driver flung back at him. "You've probably checked the books anyway, and know that. I've signed another contract with one of the petrol companies . . . their cheque's footing the bill. That's where the cash comes from, and you know it—advertising. 'Erick Millan uses Blogg's Spark Plugs' or 'Be a Millan Motorist on Tim's Tyres' and all the rest of it. But you're forgetting who gets the biggest plug of all every time I win—this firm! Every time my name's on the winning list it's 'E. Millan, Ascension Special.' Good advertising, eh? And almost free." Cold caution took control again. He let his hands fall by his side, forced a note of contrition into his next words. "I'm sorry, uncle. I didn't mean all that—but you've got to see my side."

Old Ludd kneaded his fingers one with another, face emotionless. Then, suddenly, he gave a wry smile. "I'm sorry too, boy. Listen a moment. What I'm trying to tell you is—well, if you've got worries on your mind, say the bill for these engines, for heaven's sake tell me. We're a reasonably sized business. Racing's good for prestige, too—I know that. If it helps you settle, we can afford some incidental expenses." He squared his broad, still muscular shoulders as he reached a new decision. "Look, supposing we have another talk about this after the race, maybe draw up a budget and make your team a full part of the business?"

Millan didn't rush his answer. "It might work, Uncle. It might."

"All right." Old Ludd Millan waited until the younger man had left, then rubbed one hand across his forehead, a strange, hurt expression on his face. He glanced over at the faraway wall, at the photograph of two men in army uniform, took out a handkerchief, and blew his nose with some violence.

Then, with a sigh, he turned back to the stores estimate.

Outside, Erick Millan stood by the iron balcony rail overlooking the main workshop of Ascension Motors. He scowled at the panorama of activity spread below him. Not even the squat, insectlike shapes of his two red-and-blue Ascension Specials, waiting silently in one corner, ready for their next outing, could relieve the almost vicious rage generated by the interview just completed.

The main garage area was busy. When Ascension took over the former cinema they had gutted out seating and fitments, retained only a small part of the balcony to be converted to offices, and had converted the entire stalls into a vast workshop. The stage and screen were now partitioned off as storerooms—and he watched a familiar figure emerge from the main storeroom door and walk through the ranks of assorted cars where several mechanics were busy beneath alligator-jawed bonnets.

"Hey, MacGhee." His shout was lost in the sudden clatter as a chain tackle was brought into operation, swinging a rebored engine into position over a waiting frame.

"MacGhee—" this time the man looked up. Millan pointed to the foot of the iron stairway, and swiftly clattered down the steps.

They met beside the racing cars. The bigger one, bonnet removed, the engine with its eight-in-line plug-topped cylinders stark and naked waiting the still unmounted fuel injectors, gleamed bright under the tube lights.

"Finish her off tonight, eh, Ben?" He let his fingertips run over the cold metal, metal which could come warm under his command, which would strive to breaking point if he desired.

"Should manage, Mr. Millan." Ben MacGhee was junior foreman at Ascension, but head mechanic as far as the racing team was concerned. He knew that Millan, the driver, saw the cars as power. To him, they meant something different, to be served ruthlessly in the search for mechanical perfection. When Ben MacGhee "breathed" on a machine coaxing and moulding more power and efficiency, it went far beyond valves, torque, or gear ratios. He was creating new life, fighting friction and stresses for ultimate efficiency.

Millan turned to the second car, smaller, a Maserati-based two litre designed for sports car events. Beside the other machine, with its sheer, functional G.P. lines, the sports machine might appear less exciting to the uninitiated. But it too was tuned to perfection.

"We'll do it this time," he said, eyes glinting. "Give the 'works' outfits something to think about, eh?"

MacGhee pursed his lips. "I'm still not happy about the injectors. These nozzle pressures . . ."

"Stop worrying." Millan jerked his head towards the stairway. "You sound too much like Old Ludd."

MacGhee's eyes narrowed. "Trouble again?" He licked his lips nervously. "It's not about Bell, is it?"

Millan gave a cold laugh. "Relax, Ben. The late lamented Mr. Sammy Bell was knocked down by some drunken lout who didn't stop, and died without any further stain on his character. That's official—I saw the police myself, and Old Ludd was told the same."

The workshop tannoy interrupted him, the distorted metallic voice sounding above the revving of a nearby van. "Mr. Erick Millan—telephone call, please. Mr. Erick."

There was a wall phone nearby, and he took the call there.

"Puggy here," said the voice at the other end of the line. "Got your Ford—I'm at Jacko's."

"Everything happy?" Millan asked it purely as a matter of course.

"Smooth," Puggy Carson assured him. "Hey, Mr. Millan —know something? I made forty-eight seconds."

Millan grinned. "So I should give you a medal? Right, Puggy. Wait till tonight, then move it as usual."

"To Sammy's place?"

"No—don't be a damned fool. That's finished now."

"So's Sammy," agreed Puggy. "It's a pity, Mr. Millan."

Millan became impatient. "Move the car to the other place. You're expected. Then you can get the other one around the theatre crowds and take it out to Jacko."

Puggy was satisfied. "Okay, Mr. Millan. Eh . . . what about the—"

"Cash as usual," Millan cut him short. "I'll be there tomorrow." He hung up, and turned back to his companion. "Another two in the bag by tonight," he told him.

MacGhee seemed worried. "Isn't that pushing our luck, so soon after—you know, Bell?"

"What about Bell? Changing your mind, Ben? You were the first one to tell me he'd have to go."

The mechanic reacted as if stung. "Now wait, Mr. Millan—"

"You wait," Millan told him curtly. "You know what Old Ludd just suggested? That maybe we could run the team as part of the business." He gave a snarl. "If I'm a good boy we might get a few pennies to play with. The old goat's idea of a racing budget wouldn't make you very happy, Ben. You want five thousand for your engine development, right? And that's only one item. Old Ludd would have heart failure on the spot—not that that might not be a handy situation." He tapped the fresh rubber tread of the G.P.'s tyre. "We need money, a lot of money for this, and the rest. I like money in my pocket—so do you."

The mechanic fumbled for a cigarette, then struck a match with hands which for once were not quite steady.

"We're making money, a lot of money," Millan went on remorselessly. "The whole thing's foolproof—now that Sammy Bell's been taken care of."

"Suppose they traced back?" MacGhee didn't try to hide his nervous fear.

"You know all Sammy is now?" Millan tried hard to be patient. "He's a statistic in the road accident files, one of those little pins they push into the casualty map at Police Headquarters.

"Just how we wanted it, Ben. Eh?"

CHAPTER THREE

The four P.M. tea brew at Millside police station depends for its quality on whether Joyce, the daytime switchboard operator, is having a quiet time at the board or, if she is too busy to oblige, on the marital status and domestic ability of the duty orderly who takes over the kitchen chore.

One glance at the brown liquid cooling before him, black specks of leaf gathering round the rim of the mug, showed Thane that on that particular Friday afternoon the telephone room was hard at work. Across the desk, Jock Mills sipped warily at his cup of lukewarm brew and decided that there might, after all, be worse places than a newspaper canteen—a few, anyway.

"And these are all the cuttings, eh, Jock?" Thane prodded the fat brown manilla envelope which lay before him. The *Evening Bugle* crime reporter, a familiar figure around the division, hadn't wasted time in answering their request.

"All we've got." The young reporter nodded, and waited. His fingers itched for pencil and notebook, a round dozen questions were assembled in his mind, ready to probe Thane's sudden interest in the motor racing fortunes of one Erick Millan. But he knew better than launch an attempted interview at that stage of the business. In the newspaper game a reporter stands or falls by his contacts. Jock Mills

counted his inside relationship with Colin Thane as one of
his key assets—and he wanted to keep it that way.

Thane drew out the bundle of newspaper clippings, each
neatly dated and key-marked "Erick Millan" in heavy blue
crayon. The size and variety of type faces showed that the
Bugle library cheerfully sifted rival columns to augment
its own available information. He began to read, concentrating on the print with a ferocity which ignored such
minor distractions as Jock Mills's blatant attempt to balance
a spoon on the overstrong tea and the sudden, ferocious
barking filtering through the window from the yard outside as the day's collection of stray dogs were led from the
station pound to the waiting collection van. Even Phil Moss
entering the room brought only a grunt of acknowledgment.

Moss winked at the reporter, shook his head at Jock
Mills's silent offer of a cigarette, and leaned against the
wall, letting the minutes go past.

At last, Thane looked up. "Some interesting stuff here,
Jock," he declared. "Looks as if there's pretty big money
to be earned in racing." He flipped back to one cutting.
"Listen to this, Phil. First there's starting money—paid by
the race organisers if your car even gets on to the track.
That can run up to a thousand quid on its own. If the car
wins, then there's prize money, of course—but that's postage
stamps compared with the cash income from firms who can
say you used their bits and pieces—and who'll fork out a
nice fat bonus every time you give them something to shout
about." Detective Inspector Moss, thinking of his current
bank balance and finding it considerably lacking in the
comparison, gave an appreciative whistle.

But Jock Mills shrugged. "That's only in the top bracket
—the very top," he declared. "Check the cuttings. The
motor sport boys reckon a Grand Prix win worth about five
thousand pounds to the driver. But there's maybe only a

score of championship class men in Europe who rate in that league, and a few more in the States. It seems there are hundreds of other blokes who consider they've had a lucky day if they clear their expenses and have enough left over to buy a new set of tyres." He gave a lopsided grin. "Like most other sports, it's strictly business in the top bracket—as far as the backers are concerned, anyway. I've seen our caseroom with adverts set in type, space booked for the next edition, the whole thing ready to drop into a page if the right driver wins some big event. If he does it, everybody's happy. If he loses, well, the type is thrown back into the melting pot."

"Erick Millan's finances should be fairly sound," said Moss. "He's kept himself in the winning bracket." He came over to the desk, picked up some of the discarded cuttings, and began glancing through them.

"Maybe . . ." Jock Mills hesitated, his face flushing to the roots of his carrot-red hair. "Look, Chief Inspector, I'm not asking why—not yet, anyway. But you're interested in Millan, right?"

Thane took a sip from his tea mug, found the contents now cold beyond redemption, and grimaced. "Aye, we are —but that's strictly off the record, Jock. Not even a hint at this stage."

At his side, Moss gave a sigh of mock sympathy. "Watch it, Jock. You're going to be landed in the classic situation— all you'll be able to say afterwards is that you really did know all about it, and that it wasn't your fault the opposition got the story first."

Mills gave a grunt of somewhat nervous laughter. "I'll take my chance on that. But if you're interested in Millan, it might be to do with money. . . ." He anticipated their possible reaction. "I didn't ask a question. I simply said it might be. When you phoned and asked for the cuttings you obviously weren't studying racing form. So I thought it might be a good idea to have a natter with our motoring man. Oh, I didn't tell him anything—just an afternoon's gossip between editions. Like most of our ruddy specialist writers he's got plenty of spare time on his hands. Anyway, we talked about Millan and Ascension Motors."

"The devil you did!" A mixture of surprise and interest in his voice, Thane leaned forward, elbows on his desk. "Well, what did he say?"

The reporter frowned. "There's a bit of a mystery about it all. Ascension Motors are rock-steady financially, but it seems that Old Ludd Millan and young Erick don't have quite the same views about the racing game. Erick's uncle seldom bothers to go along to see him race, and keeps him pretty tight for cash. In fact, when Erick was kicked out of the last 'works' team—everyone was polite about it, and said it was a mutual parting, but he was booted, no two ways about it—some of the wise men of the game said that he'd just disappear. Seems he tried to clobber the team manager with a monkey wrench, and the word had gone out that Millan was finished."

"But instead, he runs his own cars," prompted Thane.

"That's just it. Motor racing's an expensive hobby if you're trying for the really big time. It takes a fortune to run a racing stable." Jock Mills fumbled for a cigarette, took one from the pack extended by Thane, and accepted a light. "Thanks . . . our motoring man says you've really got to be in the millionaire class to keep in front mechanically. Seems that one of the big manufacturers pulled out of the game recently because they said their racing development section cost several hundred thousand a year to run. Well, that's major project stuff—but even keeping a couple of cars on the championship circuits might cost well into five figures." The cigarette paper had stuck to his lower lip. He probed it free from the skin with gentle care.

"Maybe it costs money, Jock, but Erick Millan is managing," said Thane softly. "Go on."

The two detectives waited, sensing the young reporter's halting explanation as a help to the crystallising of their own half-formed ideas.

Mills sighed. "That's just it, Mr. Thane. There's—well, a fair amount of cash coming in from Millan's wins. But he's not in the Stirling Moss category yet . . . despite the fact that his cars are running, that he's living it up, and that there's a strong buzz on the go that his team are building some new engine that will scare the pants off the Ferrari boys."

"Another backer maybe?" Moss raised a significant eyebrow.

"Not that anyone knows of. Millan's been interviewed, of course—but he says his plans are secret."

"Did you see this one, Colin?" Moss pushed one of the clippings along the desk. "Young Erick has fun off the track as well as on it." The photograph, taken at a nightspot table, showed the racing driver immaculate in a tartan dinner jacket, glass raised, his free hand strategically positioned round an eager, curvaceous brunette in a low-cut white cocktail dress. "Might be worth talking to her, eh?"

"Mmph." Thane had found it hard to miss the picture. "Recognise the girl?"

"Eh? Oh . . . doesn't help, does it?" Moss's enthusiasm died. The Chief Constable of their neighbour county must have been a trifle perturbed to have seen his daughter photographed in such a non-Presbyterian situation.

Jock Mills gave a grin. "There was a Chief's daughter who did things she shouldn't ought 'ter . . ." he murmured innocently.

Thane raised a hand in mock horror. "No irreverent language . . . not here, anyway," he protested. "But it points to the fact that Millan knows plenty of people who count."

"He's racing again on Sunday," volunteered the reporter. "The two Ascension Specials are entered for the Gold Helmet trophy at Charterhall. It's a race organised by some big charity outfit—proceeds in aid of medical research of some kind. Millan's one of the main draws—you won't find it in the cuttings, but he's getting seven hundred in starting money." He eyed the big detective cautiously. "How about just a wee hint? Is this big?"

Thane stroked the tip of his nose with one forefinger. Then, reluctantly, he agreed. "It could be, Jock . . . but that's all I'm telling you."

The reporter rose. "Fair enough. I won't be far away."

They waited until he had gone out and the door had closed.

Then Moss broke the silence. "Found your motive, Colin?"

"He needs the money?" Thane nodded. "It's been pretty well staring us in the face. If young Millan is running the stolen car racket, it's to get money for racing. Ach—so we've got a motive. But what else, apart from the fact that Sammy Bell worked for the firm?"

Moss shrugged. "Field, the pump man at the filling station, is in the clear," he volunteered. "Seems he was at a church guild meeting on Thursday night—and has a wife who won't even let him fill in football pools."

"Anything else?"

Moss pondered. "Sergeant MacLeod's checked in—you put him on the registration book angle, remember?"

"Any luck?" Thane doodled again on the edge of his desk blotter—row upon row of little cars. They were getting to be a habit.

"He's still working on it. Most of the write-off cars seem to have been scrapped and the registration books surrendered. He's traced a couple that were patched up—one of the new owners is threatening to sue the bloke he bought it from. Oh—and while we're at it, there's a problem in next week's duty roster. Delby and Benson are due to go on day shift—they've been on the night squad so long they're beginning to look like owls. D. C. Beech is one of the replacements, but he's screaming for a week's leave."

"His wife?" Thane grinned.

"Three o'clock this morning," agreed Moss. "Twins—a boy and a girl."

"And the best of luck," chuckled Thane with mild irony. "All right, he can have it. Ask Delby if he'll do another week. Is Beech outside?"

"Waiting and hoping."

"Get him in." Thane settled back in his chair, mind flipping back to that morning exactly ten years previous when his own first-born arrived.

Phil Moss returned a moment later shepherding the young, rather shaken Beech before him.

"Congratulations." Thane gave the new father a firm handshake. "How's the family?"

"All well, sir— I've just come from the hospital."

"All bairns look like monkeys for the first day or so," said Thane absently. "Well, when do you want this leave?"

The detective constable cleared his throat. "The hospital's a bit short of beds, sir. They suggested Monday would be a good time for her to come home."

"Three days?" It had been nearer two weeks when young Tom was born. "All right, you can stop tomorrow night. Tidy up any loose ends you can first, and let me know if you've any inquiries outstanding."

"Thanks—thanks very much, sir." The detective turned to leave.

"And Beech—"

"Sir?"

"When's the party? Must wet the baby's head—in duplicate."

"When they open. You'll be very welcome . . . sir," grinned the proud parent, striding from the room.

"That means another station whip-round," grumbled Moss, watching him go. "Weddings, christenings, hell, there's a collection sheet round every second week in this place."

"That's your ulcer talking," prodded Thane. "Or your bachelor status. When you—" the telephone's sudden clamour stopped him in mid-sentence.

He lifted the receiver. "Thane here."

The voice at the other end didn't waste words. Thane listened, then gave a growl of interest. "All right, Snouty. We'll be there. Look round tomorrow sometime." He hung up, scribbled an address on the top sheet of his deskpad, and handed it to Moss.

"The Dolman boys are going to peter a pawnshop safe tonight. Snouty thinks they'll arrive about two A.M.—the house above is empty, so it'll be another hole-in-the-ceiling job," said Thane. "Take care of it, will you, Phil?"

Moss expressed no surprise. Advance information was Snouty Leith's stock in trade. "I'll tell the uniform side to warn their beatman to keep clear," he acknowledged. "Three men and the observation van?"

Thane pondered. "Make it four. Herb Dolman's too fond of swinging an iron bar in a tight corner." He glanced at his watch. "I've some phone calls to make. We can pack it in at five, and have that quick one with Beech on the way out to my place."

There were three calls in all.

The first, inevitably, was to Buddha Ilford. The C.I.D. chief was in his office at Headquarters, and accepted Thane's progress report without comment. He did have one item of news to give in return.

"You mentioned that leak to Millan. I've located the man concerned." Buddha's tones were soft but ominous. "He goes before the Chief Constable tomorrow. We're going to roast him over a slow fire . . . though I don't think any real harm's been done."

That was Thane's own opinion. Though it didn't reduce the seriousness of the situation when a cop mentioned a possible investigation to an outside individual, Millan should still have no reason to believe that the car theft probe was in any way linked with the apparent acceptance of Sammy Bell's death as another hit-and-run motoring fatality.

He flashed the switchboard, had Joyce connect him with a florist in the city, and arranged for a large bunch of tulips to be sent to D.C. Beech's wife.

The third call was strictly business, to his opposite number in Berwickshire C.I.D. Chief Inspector Carbis at the County force's headquarters was quite willing to help.

"I want two tickets for that race meeting, Bob," said Thane. "Charterhall's within your orbit, but at the moment this is purely a Glasgow case, and one we're playing very quietly. Can you lay it on without any fuss? I want to be able to have a good look around—no official status."

Chief Inspector Carbis didn't believe in wasting time. "Hang on," he requested. Thane waited, heard him obviously speaking on another line, and then Bob Carbis was with him again.

"My golf partner's on the race committee," said the Berwickshire officer. "He can't hit a straight ball—but he can keep his mouth shut. I've got you two paddock badges. They'll take you into the pits area or anywhere else. These race committees always issue a few to friends and helpers —what's your cover, incidentally?"

Thane chuckled. "The finest in the world. A small boy who's mad-keen on motorcars."

"Tommy?" Carbis was interested. "Does he want to be a cop when he grows up?"

"He's still at the cowboys stage," said Thane thankfully.

It was just leaving six, and the sky was darkening with yet another threatened drizzle of rain. A brief visit to the pub where D. C. Beech, now more than a trifle flushed, was dispensing the customary whiskies to his C.I.D. mates, had occupied only a few minutes in the homeward journey.

Thane opened the gate at the foot of the short path leading to his front door, and ushered Phil Moss on ahead.

"Grass could do with a cut," he mused, contemplating the garden patch in the fast fading light. "Well, let's face the music."

When the house door opened, a boiling wave of shouting children seemed to pour over the two men. Tom Thane's birthday party had started off as being for himself, his young sister Kate, and a couple of school friends.

"Looks like you've got half the neighbourhood kids here, Mary," Thane greeted his wife.

"It just grew," she agreed wearily.

"Are you home for the night, Dad?" demanded the young party giver at his side. "Is that parcel for me—hello, Uncle Phil!"

"No—yes." Thane handed over the paper-wrapped bundle. "I've got to go out in a couple of hours. This is yours."

"And this—" Moss dragged another package from the pocket of his crumpled raincoat. "How's it going, young fellow?"

"Fine, thanks." The boy disappeared in a tearing of paper.

The party was an obvious success. One guest, a fat boy with glasses, was sick on the hall carpet after eating too much cake. Two others had a brief but glorious stand-up fight over whose turn it was to pin the tail on the donkey.

Young Tom had used Phil's present, a pair of toy handcuffs, to fasten his sister to the handle of the bathroom door and then had lost the key.

And the duty car called at eight exactly to take the two men back to the murder hunt. By then the drizzle which had threatened earlier had turned into pounding, battering rain, and drummed on the metal roof of the Jaguar as it headed across the city, back to South Salisbury Road, where Sammy Bell had died.

Thane wanted to see the area again by night—see it as it must have been when Sammy Bell's unconscious form had been dumped on the roadway.

The car cruised gently along the street, past the spot where Bell's body had been found, beyond the flanking engine factory, and the high, gloomy bricks of the railway boundary wall. A heavy lorry rumbled past them, travelling in the opposite direction, its headlights blazing to augment the feeble glow of the sparse scattering of streetlights.

The first sign of life in the street was about a quarter of a mile on, just where the main road swung right, leaving a small spur of cobbled surface to swing left, into the tangle of railway yards which lay beyond. A small neon sign burned brightly above the single window of the café, a dull, outwardly unattractive little shop.

"The Siding—I didn't notice that last night," said Moss.

"Probably closed. Pull in, driver," instructed Thane.

Inside, the proprietor of The Siding, a small cheerful Italian, turned from his bubbling tea-urn as the shop bell clanged.

"You want cuppa, gents? Sorry, no coffee—the machine, she's gone burst."

"Police." Thane showed his warrant card.

The Italian was unperturbed. "So?"

The café, little more than a room with three tables and an assortment of old wooden chairs, was otherwise empty.

A fat, elderly cat was stretched out asleep on the counter, its head nestling in a mound of chocolate biscuits.

"Quiet tonight, eh?" asked Moss, stroking the animal's fur.

The Italian nodded. "Trade here is just the railway shunters," he explained. "And the sometimes lorry driver. It is enough—I live."

"Stay open late?" Thane found the little man's easy-going attitude a pleasant change from the usual.

"Eleven mos' nights. The railways have tea-break at ten. Why you ask? Is it the man killed down the road las' night? I hear about it this evening. Motorcars!" He shook his head.

"We're checking on how it happened," agreed Thane. "Any strangers in yesterday evening? Any you remember?"

The man laughed. "Any stranger in here, and I remember. My customers are regular, strangers few. Yes, there was the one."

"Can you describe him?" Moss gave the cat an exploratory poke under the jaw. It opened one eye, gave him a cold glare, and went back to sleep.

The Italian spread his hands in a motion of helplessness. "Fairly young, sort of a small build, dark hair. He has three cuppas, and sits in the corner till 'bout, oh—just before the railwaymen arrive. Then he goes out—someone waits for him in a car."

"You're sure?" Thane snapped the words.

"I say so, don't I?" The Italian was puzzled. "He cannot be the one who was killed. I see the car drive up, I see this man look out the window, then he leaves my café, crosses the road—and the car drives off with him."

Moss poked the cat again, too hard this time. It spat awake, and jumped from the counter. "What kind of a car?"

The Italian shook his head. "Cars—they are all the same. I have a bicycle."

"Was it open or closed?"

"Pardon?"

Thane tried again. "Did it have a roof, or was it, you know, for the sport?"

"Ah. It had the roof," agreed the café owner.

"Damn." Moss mumbled the word."

Thane sighed. "Well, Mr.—what's your name?"

"Carutti—Alberto Carutti."

"Well, Mr. Carutti, we'll send a car round for you in the morning. We'd like you to take a look at the body in the mortuary, just in case it's the same man. All right?"

The man shrugged. "If you say. But the customer goes off in the car—how can he be knocked down in the road?"

"That's our worry, Mr. Carutti." The two detectives headed for the door.

Back in the police Jaguar, Thane asked himself the same question. If Sammy Bell was collected at ten P.M., where was he for the hour or so which followed—the hour or so until his unconscious body was dumped back in South Salisbury Road and then twice run over by the same car?

"Take her back to Millside," he told the driver. The Jaguar drew away from the kerb, while Thane sat silent, puzzling over his next move. For once, Phil wasn't talkative either. There was a rustle of paper in the darkness, then the faint, familiar sweet-sour odour of the other man's favourite brand of bismuth tablets.

"Trouble again?"

"A bit," admitted Moss. Which was a danger sign. The less Phil talked about his ulcer, the more it was bothering him.

At Millside, the car stopped, deposited its passengers, then headed round for the station yard. Once inside the main door, Moss headed for his own room, muttering that he'd be right back.

It was early yet for the night team. Their main work

began about an hour after the pubs closed. But, like divisional stations everywhere, there was plenty of activity. Only the clock on the wall and the change of faces from day-shift to night-shift officers indicated any real passage of time. A police station seldom sleeps, and when it does, there's something wrong—badly wrong.

"Looking for someone, sir?" The duty bar sergeant, his dark blue uniform brightened by two rows of medal ribbons above the left breast pocket, leaned across the heavy oak counter-top which divided the public from the private area of the main office, the counter-top from which the uniform bar got its name.

"Not just now, sergeant. Anything happening?"

The sergeant pointed a thumb towards the clock. "Friday night, sir. We've had the first of the pay-packet drunks— the main traffic will be starting soon. There's been a bit of a rammy over in Govan, though." There was a touch of near envy in his voice. "Picked up a bit on the blower— somebody was shouting how wonderful a football team the Rangers were. Then he got too personal, and a Celtic fan clattered him one with a bottle. Their pals joined in, and it needed a van load from the Govan office to sort out the battle. They've got seven of them inside. Oh, there was a teleprinter message from M.O. for you, Mr. Thane. Came in about seven—no priority. It's on your desk."

Rangers and Celtic, football and religion, drunks—well, what big city didn't have its troubles? Thane thanked the sergeant, and went upstairs.

On a sudden impulse, he stopped at Moss's office and opened the door without knocking. The thin, wiry inspector was pouring a slow-moving yellow fluid from a bottle to a tablespoon. He finished pouring, swallowed the spoonful, gave a shudder of distaste, and corked the bottle.

"Olive oil," he explained. "Hate the stuff." He belched

with eye-watering force, and blinked. "Still, controls the twinges for a bit—soothes things down."

"Look, you should see a doctor," protested Thane.

The sufferer disagreed. "I've seen plenty. Nobody's going to carve around my insides with a scalpel—not yet, anyway. Besides, I know what's up—I hate to admit it, Colin, but you can put the blame on your kid's birthday party. Two helpings of rich fruit dumpling—" he shuddered. "It'll be okay by morning."

Thane gave up. "Come on through, then."

They went through to his office. The teleprinter message was lying on the desk, as the sergeant had said. Modus Operandi somewhat apologetically reported that it had no line on file concerning any "Jacko" who had ever operated in the hot car line. It could offer a con man of that label, currently resident at Wandsworth, and a rone-pipe burglar last heard of operating in Manchester. Nothing more.

Thane took another long look at his white-faced companion.

"Let's call it a day," he decided. "Neither of us had much sleep last night. Tomorrow, I'm going to have another look around the Ascension filling stations. I want you here, Phil. Fix up a car to take our café owner to the mortuary, try and get a fresh line on this Jacko character—he's still the only outside link we've got with Bell—and then draw up a really detailed listing of stolen cars for, let's see, the last two weeks anyway. Okay?"

Phil Moss ran one rather shaky hand through his thinning hair. He was about to protest, then changed his mind. "Thanks, Colin."

"For what?" Thane reached for his hat.

The radio was busy as they left the building.

"Cars one-five and two-one, Sauchiehall Street at Charing Cross, man reported brandishing a bayonet," said the calm, impersonal voice of the Headquarters controller. "Sauchie-hall Street at Charing Cross. Beatman also attending."

"Dear old Glasgow town," muttered Thane.

He meant it too—but you'd have to be born in the place to understand why.

Eight A.M. on a Saturday morning was an unusual time for Puggy Carson to be out and about. But, for a change, the sun was shining bright in the sky, the radio weather forecast said that conditions should hold for a spell, and there was only a little job of work remaining before he collected cash for the previous day's business.

Washed, shaved, as neatly dressed as ever, Puggy left the South Side boardinghouse where he was "Mr. Carson—a salesman who has to work such late hours" and caught a trolley-bus into the city. He changed buses in Argyle Street, smoked a cigarette as the vehicle swept silently along, and got off at a stop only a couple of minutes' walk from Jacko Menran's place in Peaceview Terrace.

Puggy strolled up the short, ash-covered lane which led from the tenement street to the back yard hut, its double doors shut and locked. He listened a moment, heard the faint sounds of activity within, and decided he had time for a spot of fun at the expense of his normally dismal-spirited companion.

One fist hammered hard three times on the wooden door-jamb. "Open up, Menran. We know you're in there."

There was a sudden, muffled curse from within, the clatter of metal on metal.

Puggy relented. "Relax, Jacko, it's only me."

He had to wait a full minute before the door swung open and Jacko looked out, eyes darting around. The other man scowled. "You stupid, nit-brained—"

"Ach, forget it, Jacko," said Puggy. "Just a joke . . . that's all."

Jacko lowered the heavy mallet held ready in one hand. "Come in, and shut the door behind you."

Puggy sauntered through, and obeyed.

"Come to collect the car," he said, perching himself on the workbench within and helping himself to a cigarette from a packet lying amid the tools. "Got a light?"

"Matches beside the spray gun," growled Jacko.

"Ta. How's it coming?" Puggy gave the car an interested inspection. It was a small shooting brake, finished, as he'd been instructed, in apple-green. "First of that type I've tackled," he said. "Couldn't slide the window with the sucker, and had to knock the lock off the rear door. Threw my timing right out—lucky the old car park geezer had toddled off for a quick 'un."

Jacko turned from his inspection of a buffed-down portion of the car's engine block. "I know that," he said bitterly. "Took me over an hour to fix the mess. Then there were two bits of paintwork which needed patched up . . . somebody'd simply gone over them with a touch-up brush."

"It's the poor light at night," protested Puggy. "You can't spot everything . . . it's all right for you, mate. You stay here nice and cozy and just wait till the cars come in. Then all you've got to do is stick on a few things like wing mirrors and wheel discs, change around spot lamps or seat covers, and tart the thing up so nobody recognises it. But I'm the bloke that goes out and gets it—remember that. I'm the bloke that runs the real risk of landing in the dock."

Jacko sneered. "Belt up. You get your dough. Here, come and hold this lamp steady while I use the teeper."

Puggy's good humour had gone. But he obeyed while the mechanic brought over the small box of metal die stamps and the teep—a small, punch-like tool with a hollow nose. He rubbed his fingertips once again over the spot where the original engine number had been buffed away, selected the first die he required, slipped it into the teep nose, and raised his hammer.

It took about ten minutes' work, changing from die to die, positioning the teep, then striking hard with the hammer, to substitute the new six-figure engine number. Jacko inspected the finished job, rubbed a heavy mixture of oil-soot over the bright metal, and was satisfied.

"That's her ready," he declared. "Hell, no, I forgot the speedo. Bring over the drill while I drop the cable."

"Okay." Puggy went over to the workbench, checked that the small electric hand drill was plugged in to the mains, and trailed the cable over.

Down on his back on the car floor, head and hands under the dashboard, his companion removed the drive cable from the speedometer head, then felt blindly for the drill. Puggy placed it in his hand.

"Tip's on," he confirmed.

The drill's normal steel cutting head had been replaced by what looked like a blunt knitting needle with a flattened point. The point was fed into the drive slot.

"She's at eleven thousand," said Jacko. "We'll take it back to five." He pressed the drill's starter trigger.

Turning at several thousand revs per minute, the drill-head sent the figures of the mileage recorder spinning crazily forward. Still the drill whined, while Jacko's muscles cramped. Fifty . . . seventy . . . eighty-five . . . ninety-five thousand miles were recorded. Then, the number bands exhausted, the recorder suddenly registered a row of zeroes and began building up from scratch.

"Easy," cautioned Puggy, shouting above the whine of the drill. "She's coming up. Four . . . four five—cut it now!"

The drill was silenced. Jacko reinserted the speedo drive cable and secured it down before he crawled out and permitted himself the luxury of a stretch.

"Four thousand eight hundred. A bit low. Still, what the hell, it's only supposed to be about seven months old. So it had a careful driver."

Puggy Carson prowled round the car. "What did she need?"

"Apart from the door lock?" Jacko pondered. "New pedal rubbers and carpets, of course. Seats were okay—I ditched the covers. New set of country-type tyres on the back, substitute wing mirrors, couple of spot lamps on front, some other bits and pieces. Oh, and a couple of travel pennants on the rear window. Now take it away, will you? I've been up all night—I need sleep."

They opened the double doors. Puggy started the motor, and backed the shooting brake out along the lane. Jacko ignored his wave of farewell.

From Peaceview Terrace to the car's destination was only about half an hour's drive through the heavy traffic. Puggy was at ease, even when he had to halt only a few feet away from a points policeman—who without any doubt at all had a full description of the car he was driving and its former registration number listed in his notebook along with the rest of the day's "lookout requested" instructions from morning muster.

The car's owner could have walked round it and been none the wiser . . . which was why Jacko Menran drew a higher percentage than Puggy when it came to carving up the profits.

Bacarro Motors, Ltd., was situated in Kempville Street, at the start of the city's suburban fringe. It wasn't big as motor showrooms go—at one time it had been the site of a funeral undertaker's business. But people round about had been unusually healthy. He'd gone burst—and now the showroom, with about a dozen cars displayed behind its broad plate-glass windows, stood in its place.

Puggy Carson steered the shooting brake to the building's rear entrance, parked beside a familiar little red-and-blue sports car, and went inside. The duty salesman gave him a nod of recognition, and nodded towards the small frosted-glass office.

"They're waiting."

He knocked on the office door, and strode in.

Erick Millan and another man were in the room, sitting side by side at a small table, papers spread before them.

"Everything okay, Puggy?" asked Millan, pulling a bulky envelope from one pocket of his sheepskin jacket.

"It's outside," agreed Puggy. "How's business, Liscomb?"

Liscomb, sleek, balding, with a neat hairline moustache, smirked. "Selling not too badly."

Liscomb completed the setup. As front-man and manager of Bacarro Motors, he was accepted by his staff of three as the boss. Inevitably, they realised that Millan was also involved—"something he wants to keep quiet about, just remain a sleeping partner," was Liscomb's explanation to the trio, who also accepted Puggy Carson as a touring buyer, and had no idea that every day of their lives they were involved in selling a brisk line in stolen cars.

"Why the paperwork?" asked Puggy, pointing to the table. "Ta—" he caught the envelope as it was tossed across by Millan, didn't bother to count the contents, and shoved it into his breast pocket.

"Working out some prices," said Millan, rising. "How about a drink, Liscomb?"

The front-man opened a cupboard, produced a bottle and glasses, and poured.

"It's difficult, Puggy," said Millan. "You see—thanks—" he took the offered glass, tasted the whiskey, then took a longer gulp. "We've got to keep prices right. Keen enough to attract the customers, yet not too low or we'll have the rest of the trade smelling a rat."

"What about this saloon—the one Puggy brought in last

night?" Liscomb pursed his lips. "The guide lists it at seven-fifty."

Millan pondered. "Mark it seven hundred and thirty pounds," he decided. "Try the shooting brake at eight hundred. Anything else?"

"Well . . . " Liscomb broached his subject with care. "How many cars are coming in next week?"

"Five if you've got the space," said Millan.

The front-man shook his head. "Things have been slow this week, you know that from the figures. Besides, I got landed with three trade-in cars in part exchange."

"Get rid of them at an auction," snapped Millan. "Two of them, anyway. Keep the best—it'll look more natural to these characters on the floor. And we'll cut back to four deliveries."

Liscomb drained his glass. "What I really meant was, well, what about Sammy Bell?"

"What about him?" Millan froze a little.

"Now he's dead—what happens? Won't the police be around? According to the papers they didn't trace the driver."

Millan relaxed. "That? All that happens is that we can't use the filling station for a spell."

"You'll be working someone else in," suggested Puggy. "To take his place—now I know a boy who might do. He's young, but he's smart. You'll need someone, Mr. Millan. Heck, I don't mind lifting more cars for a spell, but there's a limit to luck—anyway, I could use a break. I've a roll of dough waiting to be spent."

"Leave the thinking to me," said Millan softly, fastening the sheepskin round him. "Bell was another of your bright boys, Puggy, remember? He didn't work out, did he?" He went over to the door, then turned, a deceptive smile on his face. "It's a pity they can't find the driver, isn't it?"

The door slammed behind him. The two men in the room didn't move for a moment. Then Liscomb gave a shaky laugh. "I could use another drink."

He headed towards the bottle.

Millan drove his Sprite up the short sloping ramp from street level, stopped with a squeal of brakes beside the reception area, and jumped out, leaving the car's engine ticking.

"Park her for me," he told the Ascension garage hand who came over.

The man grinned. "Ready for tomorrow, sir?"

Millan gave him a wink. "Give me a dry track, and we'll take the pants off anything we come up against."

He walked over the concrete, up to the far corner of the garage. The big transporter bus, finished in the team's red-and-blue colours, its sides covered with money-making petrol and tyre adverts, was backed into position, broad tailboard lowered ready to receive the two waiting race cars.

Ben MacGhee was there, checking over a list of equipment as it was stored aboard by the two other team mechanics who'd be travelling with them to Charterhall. MacGhee watched the two gas cylinders for the portable welding rig loaded aboard, ticked them off his list, then turned. "All set to load, Mr. Millan."

The racing driver and his head mechanic stood together, each gaining separate satisfaction from the sight of the waiting cars.

"Mind you," said MacGhee cautiously, "I'd have liked a wee bit more time on the big 'un's injectors."

Millan brushed it aside. "You spent three hours on it last night, Ben. I'm satisfied . . . and I do the driving. If I left it to you, you'd still be changing ideas right up to the starter's flag. Load 'em."

The silent, gleaming cars possessed a surprising amount of weight. Millan joined the mechanics in the muscle-straining effort required to push first the two-litre sports car and then the bigger racing machine up the gleaming metal track of the tailboard. MacGhee left the other two men to lash down the cars, ready for their journey, and joined Millan outside the transporter.

"I've just been at Liscomb," said Millan, wiping sweat from his brow. "Carson was there—he moved the shooting brake."

MacGhee glanced nervously at the two men working nearby.

"Relax," said Millan impatiently. "You'll be jumping at your own shadow before long. What's your worry?"

The overalled mechanic lowered his voice to a near whisper. "It's your uncle. There was a detective out this morning—they were in his office for nearly half an hour."

"Damn. What did he want?"

"I don't know. They came over here on the way out, and stopped for a look at the cars. The detective—Thane his name was—said he was taking his youngster to Charterhall tomorrow."

"Thane?" Millan snapped finger and thumb. "I met him at the filling station. Probably still checking on Sammy Bell."

"But why here?"

The racing driver didn't hide his impatience. "Because Bell worked for us, you fool. Stick to your engines, Ben."

The mechanic shook his head. "I'm worried. Did you—" he stopped.

"Did I what?"

"Nothing, Mr. Millan. I'll make sure the cars are properly bedded."

Millan nodded. "Do that. I'll go and talk to Old Ludd. Find out what this fellow Thane was after."

Ludd Millan was in his office, dictating a letter. He finished it, the secretary left in a swish of pleated skirt, and the older man leaned back in his chair. "All ready to go, Erick?"

"I've just finished helping to load them," confirmed his nephew. "Ben says the police were here. Was it about Bell?"

"Aye. It was that Chief Inspector—the one you told me about. They don't seem to be getting very far with it. He wanted to know if there was any reason why Bell should have been in South Salisbury Road—in case it might help them find a witness." He frowned down at the desk surface, fingers toying with a short stub of pencil. "You know, Erick, I don't think they'll ever find out who was responsible." He looked up. "Do you?"

"Me?" Moving over to the window, the younger man stood with his back to the desk. "I suppose not. The drunk who hit him's probably quivering at home somewhere, and having a fainting fit every time there's a knock on the door."

Behind him, he heard a sigh. He didn't bother to turn. There was a girl walking along the street outside. A very pretty girl, blonde. He watched her till she disappeared round the corner.

At that particular moment, Detective Inspector Phil Moss was also concerned with women . . . one in particular. He'd have sacrificed a year's pension rights to have her say good-bye and leave him in peace. Not that his ulcer was troubling him—the night's rest, plus further heavy doses of olive oil had left him with a distinct lack of appetite but otherwise little aftereffects.

"It's so easy talking to you," cooed Ida Murdock. "I feel —well, that you understand these things. So strange you never married—just like me, Inspector."

"As you say," he agreed wearily. "Now, let me get this right, Miss Murdock . . ."

"Ida," she protested coyly. "I get shivers when people call me Miss Murdock. When it's a policeman, I think I'm going to be arrested. Your first name's Philip, isn't it? Do they call you Phil?"

"Sometimes." Moss was growing more desperate. This plump, middle-aged woman before him had a persistence which was frightening. Gone were the slacks and jersey of the previous day. Ida Murdock was tightly corsetted into a blue linen dress with a startling neckline. The hat on her head was crowned by a single massive imitation cherry, hanging on the end of a slender wire stalk. Every time her head moved the cherry began bobbing in hypnotic fashion. "Now look, Miss—Ida, let me make sure of this. Your brother's quite positive that John Carner's working at this address."

She nodded, and the cherry danced dizzily. "Sam spent most of last night phoning his friends. Sam's got a good name in the trade, you know, despite that trouble we had. Anyway, Phil, there you are. The other man you wanted to know about has emigrated." She let loose her incongruous giggle. "We knew it was important to you, and Sam's so busy just now—so I just said I'd bring it in myself. And, well," she beamed. "Here I am. Is this your room?"

"No. It's Chief Inspector Thane's," said Moss, falling back on stiff formality as a desperate defence. "Well, it was kind of you to come—a phone call would have done."

"Telephone?" she was horrified. "No, I was sure you'd prefer me to come personally . . . and I'm glad I did. There's such an atmosphere about the place . . ."

"That's the disinfectant," said Moss apologetically. "They give the corridors an extra scrub-down on Saturdays."

She laughed, waving a podgy forefinger almost under his nose. "That's not what I meant, and you know it, too.

Now, when will we hear what happens? You'll be coming
out again soon, won't you?"

"We can't. . . ."

Ida Murdock hung her head. "Of course, it may be
secret—that was silly. But still, you can come as a friend,
Phil. Now you won't be on duty on Sunday afternoon, I
know. I asked that nice young detective with the new
babies when I was waiting to see you—he told me. I won't
have you just sitting in some boardinghouse by yourself.
Besides," her light blue eyes swept him, "some good home
cooking wouldn't do you any harm. As I always say to Sam,
men just don't know how to look after themselves."

"But . . ."

The podgy finger wagged again. "That's settled. You can
come and talk to my brother about motorcars. I'll make a
special fruit dumpling."

Moss felt suddenly weak. Ida Murdock rose, clutching
her massive handbag. "Well, I must run now. A girl must
get her shopping done, you know."

He saw her out, then came back and slumped down in
the chair, suddenly exhausted. Outside, in the main C.I.D.
room, Detective Constable Beech worked on, unaware of
the fact that only his new-born twins were saving him from
a fate close to summary execution.

"Portrait of a man at work." Thane stood in the still open
doorway, a grin on his face. "Bumped into Ida Murdock
on the way out. Twittered that she'd given you some information."

Moss groaned. "She gave me more than that."

Thane shut the door, hung his hat on the peg, and gazed
at him, still grinning. "Don't know what the women see in
you, Phil. Did you tell her what an Inspector's pay amounts
to?" He backed away in mock alarm. "It's a serious offence
to strike a superior officer."

"Dry up," growled Moss. "She's fixed me to go out to her

place tomorrow—unless I can think of a good enough reason to put it off. That woman's a menace."

"Ach, she's goodhearted enough." Thane took his now vacated chair. "What did she have to tell, anyway?"

"Her brother's located Carner. He's working in a showroom near Bothwell Street."

"Big John, eh?" Thane was interested. "Anything else?"

"I've drafted out that table of stolen cars you wanted." Moss passed over two close-ruled sheets. "There were another seven cases yesterday. Four were found abandoned later on, the Dolman boys were using another for transport when they were picked up. . . ."

"Any trouble?"

"None. They arrived at the pawnshop just as Snouty forecast. Our boys gave them fifteen minutes, then moved in—the Dolmans had the safe primed, ready to blow."

"Even with a good lawyer, they'll draw five years apiece," said Thane grimly. The Dolmans had been a thorn in the Millside Division, and would be again in all probability once they got out. But even with the usual remission, their coming sentence would make things quieter for a spell. "That leaves three cars."

"One was seen heading south on the Carlisle road. North of England's been advised. The other two, well, they've vanished. A saloon yesterday afternoon, and a shooting brake last night," said Moss, checking his other list. "Oh, and that Italian from the café was at the mortuary this morning. He's not positive, but he thinks Sammy was his customer."

It was difficult to identify Sammy. Even his brother had admitted that when he'd seen the smashed face. There's a lot of weight above a car tyre.

The Scientific Bureau had weighed in with another contribution. Dan Laurence's terse message said that microscopic examination of the cement grit on the dead man's shoes had yielded one interesting result. The grit included sand particles from the original concrete mix. "Particles included high count of crushed shell to uncommon degree, suggesting beach sand from South West England. Endeavouring to trace."

Thane lifted one foot, and squirmed in his chair to examine the sole of his shoe. The leather was clean.

"The Ascension place has a concrete floor. It's worth a try— I saw Beech outside, didn't I?"

"You did." Moss was still bitter.

"Tell him to go out there on some excuse—he wants to buy a can of oil, anything—and make sure he gets some of that grit on his shoes. After that, he's to get straight back in the car, take the things off, and go to Laurence at Headquarters. He can pad around in his socks till they've got the scrapings. Okay?"

"It's a pleasure."

Thane lifted the phone. "I'm going to check in with Buddha. I'd a talk with Ludd Millan—and if you ask me, he's on edge about something. My bet is he's more than a little worried about his nephew. Oh—and get the car round, Phil. I think we should go and have a word with Big John Carner."

The pub was a quiet one, just across the road from the showroom. Big John Carner, mild enough in his dark suit, white collar, and quiet tie, took a long drink from his beer, smacked his lips, and laid the glass down on the marble-topped corner table.

"It's better in here," he said. "And thanks—my boss wouldn't be very happy if it looked as if I was being grilled in front of customers."

Moss nursed a tonic water, content to leave the talking to Thane. After all, he could always phone the woman, and

say he'd been called out on an inquiry . . . though she'd
probably try again.

"We never had enough on you, Carner—not enough for
the courts, anyway," said the Chief Inspector. "You've been
with the same firm for the last three years. . . ."

"And working for a living," the other man concluded for
him. "Ask who you want, I don't mind. Look, I've got a
family now, and a building society loan. If I see the odd
characters I used to know, I head the other way, fast. I
got one hell of a fright over that Murdock business, a big
enough fright to get out. I stayed in the car trade because
it's the only one I know—and anyway, I like it."

"What's your job?"

"Me?" Carner chuckled. "I'm a bowler hat man—for the
moment anyway, then it'll be somebody else's turn." He
enjoyed the puzzlement that caused, took another gulp of
beer, and explained. "It's part of the game, see. Every now
and again when we sell a car we've got to take in some old
banger in part exchange. It's a liability—that's where the
bowler hat man comes in. Maybe we've got a customer
who's looking for a particular car—must be the right shade,
that sort of thing. We haven't got one, but we know another outfit who have. They may be on the other side of
the city, or in another town—that's part of the job too,
knowing who's got what. Follow me?"

Both detectives showed the necessary appreciation.

"Right. So I put on my hat—though it isn't a bowler—
and I drive off in the old banger. I'm just a customer in
from the street as far as the other lot are concerned. I say I
want to buy their car, I don't quibble about the price, but
I've got my old faithful motorcar outside—they'll have to
take that as part of the deal, and I want a good trade-in
value for it. Maybe it trims their profit, but it's a sale, so
what the hell. We get rid of the banger for more than we
had to pay for it, we've got the other car we were after, a

good 'un that we can sell with a good guarantee about condition, the customer is so pleased that he's ready to pay a little extra over the odds, and everybody's happy."

"Except the firm who have the banger," said Moss sardonically.

Carner winked. "It's a merry-go-round, Inspector. They probably have a bowler-hat man too. One we don't know. It's all part of the business."

Thane swirled his glass. "We're looking for someone, Carner. He could be working around the trade, we don't know. There have been too many cars disappearing lately, and he may know some of the answers. Ever heard of a man named Jacko?"

"Jacko?" Carner rested his chin on one hand. "Rings a bell, but it's going back a bit." He hesitated. "Jacko—I don't want to get involved in anything, Mr. Thane. The boss wouldn't like it—he doesn't know about, well, how I . . . you know."

"Just a name, you finish your beer, and we say good-bye," Thane told him.

Carner drummed an uncertain tattoo on the tabletop.

"Of course, if we found out later that you had known, but didn't tell us, that could amount to hindering an investigation." The Chief Inspector's meaning was clear.

The car salesman laid his hand flat on the marble. "All right. There's Jacko Menran. When I knew him he was a fixer—probably still is. He's got a place over in Partick." He patted his pockets. "Got a cigarette?"

Thane handed him a pack. Carner took one, lit it, drew deep. "I met him just after the war, when the world was hungry for anything with wheels and the clever characters were making a killing. All a car had to do was look good, and Jacko made sure it did. You know the sort of thing— take an old banger on its last legs, pour sawdust into the gearbox and metal compound in the back axle to cut down the noise, heavy oil in the sump to stop the big-ends knock-ing—maybe even saw-cut new treads on the tyres if they were too bald. Jacko knew it all, and little extras like how to keep the tyre pressures down to hide body rattles. Give him some brown paper, a tube of metallic cement and a spray gun and he could hide any amount of rust. 'Course, they caught up with some of the clever boys, but not with Jacko—he never sold cars. He simply did the work and got paid.

"I'm not saying he touched much stolen stuff. But if anybody wanted a good fixer, Jacko'd be the answer."

Peaceview Terrace is in the Marine Division. Twenty minutes after Thane had found Menran Auto Electrics listed in the phone book, two plain-clothes men began a constant watch on the battered back yard hut. Their van-tage point was a tenement window two storeys up. One had binoculars. Both had orders to note full details of all visitors or cars arriving. But they—and the men who were to relieve them later—were under emphatic instruction to do nothing else, no matter the circumstances.

Phil Moss was on his way to visit the governor at Barlinnie Prison, where Sammy Bell had served his last term. Sammy had had to be contacted somewhere along the line, recruited into the car-stealing setup. If the name of Menran was listed in the visiting day columns, another portion of the story would be known.

Slowly, the mills were beginning to grind.

CHAPTER FOUR

Detective Constable Beech straightened his tie, knocked a trifle nervously on the door marked "Chief Inspector," and went in.

"It's me, sir."

Thane initialled the last of the bundle of C.I.D. expense sheets, tossed them into the wire "Out" basket, and glanced at his watch. "Four o'clock . . ."

"I'm just going, sir—on leave." Beech cleared his throat. "My wife liked the flowers—she asked me to thank you."

"Not every day we get twins in the division." Thane folded his arms, and sat back. "What the devil's that on your feet?"

Beech was more embarrassed than ever. He wriggled his toes inside the oversized white tennis sandals. "The Scientific Bureau kept my own shoes, sir. Superintendent Laurence wanted them for the garage grit. I borrowed these from Sergeant MacLeod—he had them in his desk."

"Hmm." At times Dan Laurence could have a peculiar sense of humour. Thane dropped the subject. "Any work outstanding?"

"I've cleared up most of the inquiries, sir." Beech handed him a thin folder. "Only these three left. One's a shoplifting—the main witness is on holiday till next Wednesday. The other two are cranks, but I thought I'd better leave a note about them in case they showed up again. The first one says a Russian spy's after him with a death ray, but he's a harmless old character."

"The complainer, or the spy?" The junior d.c. in any division always gets the nuisances to dispose of—it's as inevitable as an initiation ceremony.

"The complainer, sir." D.C. Beech was long since immune to the wit of senior officers. "The other case is a man who wants us to help him sue a firm—I suggested he contact a solicitor."

The telephone rang. Thane put down the file, and lifted the receiver. Covering the mouthpiece with one hand, he told the youngster, "Well, get going—and good luck." As Beech left, Thane took the call. Phil Moss was on the line.

"I'm just leaving Barlinnie," said Moss. " 'Fraid we're out of luck here—I've been through the visiting lists, and if Jacko Menran ever came to see Bell he didn't use his real name."

"Did Bell have many visitors?"

Moss's voice crackled on the line. "About half a dozen, including his brother who came once. I've got the names, but they mean nothing. Usual lodginghouse addresses. Want me to come straight back?"

Thane pondered the point. "No, call in at Headquarters first, and see if you can get the result of that comparison test Dan Laurence is running for us on the grit samples. And try and get young Beech's shoes, will you? Laurence sent him back in his stocking soles."

Moss chuckled, and agreed. Thane replaced the phone, lit a cigarette, and once again began reading the wad of newspaper cuttings from the *Bugle* library. Some of the accompanying illustrations were interesting. Millan at Nurburgring, Millan after a crash at Monza, another one of him winning the British Grand Prix, that familiar, fresh-faced

smile shown to full advantage as he sat in the cockpit of
the car, surrounded by his pit crew and admirers. Thane
recognised one of the faces—Ben MacGhee, the head mechanic whom he'd seen at the Ascension garage that
morning.

On an impulse, he took the cutting from the bundle,
folded it, and put it in his inside pocket.

The phone rang again. It was one of the plain-clothes
watchers at Peaceview Terrace. "Changing over shifts, sir,"
he reported. "Hasn't been much activity so far. We've
identified Menran through the householder who's co-
operating. He left the garage about half an hour ago, and
locked up behind him. We got a reasonable observation
when the doors were being opened and closed—the place
seems to be empty. Menran uses a motorcycle, a big twin-
cylinder job. We've got the licence number."

There wasn't much else to do. It was the time Thane
hated most in an investigation, the time when he knew he
was beginning to make progress, but progress which was
slow and which couldn't be forced to a faster pace.

Phil Moss brought matters on a little. The lean, thin-
faced detective thumped a brown paper parcel on Thane's
desk the moment he arrived, and announced: "Beech's
boots. And here's the report that goes with them."

Thane snatched the paper, sensing the other man's half-
hidden enthusiasm. He read it through, then thumped the
desktop. "The samples match. Same shell sand and traces
of motor oil. Even the oil's a similar grade."

"Aye." Moss hefted the parcel containing Beech's foot-
wear. "They're still working on where the sand came from.
As far as they can trace, there's only one firm shipping
supplies into the area. It's used for ready-mixed concrete
—you know, delivered wet by the lorryload. Shipments began
about four years ago."

Several hundred building sites in the city might have

that particular concrete embodied in their structure. A few might be garages or other places where there might be oil traces. A smaller number might have the same spectroscopic blending of oil. As evidence, any Queen's Counsel might shoot it full of holes. But to Thane it represented a justification.

"You're going to Berwickshire tomorrow," said Moss. "What about this end?"

"I know what I'd like you to do," growled Thane. "That's check the underside of every car young Millan's driven in the last few days. The car that killed Sammy Bell will still have blood and other bits of human debris clinging to it, no matter how good a try there's been at cleaning. But we can't do that—not yet."

"We could run a full check on his movements—at least find out if he's got an alibi lined up," protested his companion.

"How?" Thane grimaced. "Any move like that, and we bring it out into the open that this is a murder investigation. You know what happens then—the car ring scatters, or at least shuts down. We've got to get both birds with the one stone, and we're still trying to find the ruddy stone."

Moss popped a bicarbonate tablet into his mouth, and began to suck. "Jock Mills could do it," he said slowly. "A reporter building up a feature on the life of a racing driver. Millan likes publicity—the cuttings prove it. Jock could barge in almost anywhere—friends, relations, ask questions, and squeeze out what we want in the process."

The Millside chief sat silent, digesting the idea. He trusted Jock Mills, and the fact that the situation wasn't in the rulebook didn't particularly worry him. But there had to be a condition: "See if he'll do it . . . though he's got to understand that there's no story about it afterwards. Officially, we don't know a thing about what he's up to.

Tell him to keep in touch with you—no, blast, you're on day-off, aren't you?"

Moss dead-panned. "I don't mind. Of course, I'll need to phone Miss Murdock and disappoint her, but—" he winked.

Charterhall race track lies near Greenlaw, in Berwick-shire, just over eighty miles from Glasgow. An R.A.F. fighter-training aerodrome built in World War II, converted into a motor racing venue by Scots enthusiasts some ten years later, it still remains the country's only genuine car racing circuit, a fast two miles to the lap of tarmac formed from now disused runways and taxiing apron.

For Thane, driving down in a small saloon drawn from the Traffic garage pool, his young son bubbling with excitement by his side, the journey amounted to a steady three hours' motoring, part of it in long, slow-moving convoy as race-fans' cars by the thousand began to clog the narrow country roads leading to the circuit.

The weather was continuing its shift towards summerlike conditions, hot, warm, and with little wind . . . ideal for the normally quiet farming district, with its rich earth and lush green fields. But he didn't envy the County police details their jobs as they stood, white-gloved and perspiring, struggling to keep the flow of traffic moving, helping to extricate the occasional local who made a determined effort to force his battered truck or van clear of the throng and off into some more sedate side road.

"We're there, Dad!" Young Tom, still hardly believing his luck, bounced in the seat as he caught a first glimpse of the yellow direction signs and the army of cars parked beyond.

Thane followed the traffic ahead, swung off the road, bounced down the narrow, dusty track past disused brick and iron buildings left over from the former service days, then pulled in beside the small police tent.

"Wait in the car—and don't move," he warned his son.

Chief Inspector Carbis had kept his promise. Two paddock tickets were waiting, plus a car park sticker; their passports into the inner circle within the track circuit, Charterhall's holy of holies containing the behind-the-scenes of racing seldom glimpsed by the spectators who lined the outer boundaries of the two-mile distance or who sat in sheltered but hard-chaired splendour in the four specially erected grandstands.

The car pass displayed on his windscreen, Thane tucked in at the tail of a troop of racing tenders, a petrol tanker, and an ambulance, followed them across the still silent track, and was waved on to the small parking area set aside by the charities group for officials and those wealthier visitors who were prepared to dig deep into their wallets in the cause of medical research and some close-up views of racing machinery.

Stopped between a silver-grey Bentley and a massive left-hand-drive Cadillac, Thane pulled on the handbrake. "Now listen, young fellow," he instructed his son. "You don't move a yard away from my side, you don't touch anything unless I say so, and you keep that autograph book in your pocket unless I give you the okay. Understood?" The boy nodded solemnly, and Thane reached out to rumple his hair. "Come on then, let's see what this racing's about."

The first two races were minor five-lap affairs for production sports machines, intended as a warm-up for the main events to come.

As the second stream of brightly painted small cars jostled out on to the starting grid the Thanes turned from their vantage point and began to walk down the length of the central paddock area.

On all sides engines snarled in monotonous chorus, throttles blipped by white overalled mechanics as their precious charges were warmed and adjusted to hairsbreadth degrees, ready for the straining miles ahead. Beside some cars, drivers were in earnest consultation. Others, mainly the visiting Continental stars with a bronzed line in Riviera sun tan, stayed aloof. Niccolo, the works Ferrari ace who'd notched fastest time in practice, gaining first place in the grid for the coming Formula One race, relaxed in a sky-blue canvas armchair placed under a rainbow-hued canopy. His interpreter was nearby, an ice-cooled bottle was at his side, and Niccolo obviously wanted to be alone.

"Look, Dad—there's Erick Millan!" The boy's voice was shrill with excitement. Thane followed his awe-struck gaze.

The big transporter, its two cars disgorged, stood only a few yards distant. The blue-and-red Ascension Specials sat side by side, mechanics busy at the rear-mounted engine of the bigger machine. Dressed in a red-and-blue one-piece overall, elasticised at the wrists and waist, the trouser legs tucked into ankle-length racing slippers, Millan stood over them. Flanked on either side by an admiring group of tweedy enthusiasts, he seemed amused by one comment, replied with a white-toothed grin, then for the first time caught sight of Thane. Slapping one of the mechanics on the back, Millan strode over.

"Hardly recognised you, Chief Inspector—" he gestured at the detective's week-end rig of slacks and sports jacket. "My uncle mentioned you might be down. This your boy?"

Thane nodded. "Making our first visit to a motor race. Having trouble?"

"That?" Millan waved the matter aside. "They decided they want to change a couple of plugs—as far as they're concerned, I only drive the thing." Behind him, the eight cylinders burst into life. "Well, I'd better get back—enjoy yourselves."

Thane watched him go and his eyes were suddenly bleak

as he saw the embryo racing idol rejoin the party round the car.

"Dad . . ." he felt a tug on his sleeve. "You didn't introduce me," complained his son. "An' I wanted his autograph."

"Later, maybe," he promised. "Come on, let's have a look at that car across the way. I think it's a Cooper—we haven't seen one of them yet."

Obediently, the boy followed.

The first of the two main races of the day—and Millan's opening appearance—was the twenty-lap event for un-limited-power sports cars. Heading for a trackside vantage point, close by the Ascension pits, the Thanes arrived in the final still seconds before the fall of the starter's flag. Cars lined up on one side of the tarmac, drivers poised and ready opposite for the traditional Le Mans-type start—the vast crowd seemed hardly to breathe. Then down fell the Union Jack flag, the crash-helmeted drivers sprinted car-wards—Millan's blue-and-red overalled figure full seconds ahead—doors slammed, there was a sudden, staccato firing of engines, and the cars were off, howling down the three-quarter mile straight, disappearing round the first bend in a crescendo of gear-changing revs and a squealing of tyres. The Ascension Special was already ahead as the first drivers entered the long reverse curve of the circuit, their cars moving streaks against the dark tarmac.

"You're a stranger," murmured a voice in Thane's ear.

One hand still firm on his son's shoulder, the detective turned, then gave a warm handshake to the man who had spoken.

"Dan Beauman. What the devil brings you here?" he demanded.

Beauman, once a Manchester C.I.D. sergeant, flipped his lapel to show the small silver badge below.

"Track security. Well, that's the publicity line, anyway

. . . my firm's simply keeping an eye on the cash that's
been paid in. We've got an armoured van parked somewhere, ready to cart the money off to the bank. There's
about sixty thousand quid in drawings from this lot." The
security man beamed with pleasure. "It's nice to see you.
How's the family—"

A thunderous roar as the lead cars shot past the pits,
Millan leading, drowned his next words. As the last car
receded, he tried again. "How's the family, Colin? All well
at home? Hey—is this Tom? He was only about three the
last time I saw him."

"Be about that," agreed Thane. Twice he and Dan Beauman had been involved in cases together. On top of that,
they'd once found themselves on a fortnight's holiday at
the same Cornish seaside hotel.

While the youngster's attention remained fixed on the
race, the two men gossiped.

"Why did I pack in the force?" Beauman became more
serious. "Money, Colin—nothing else. I'm one of what the
chief constables call the percentage wastage, a trained man
who packs in long before he reaches pension age. Sometimes
I wish I hadn't—but there's still twice as much money in my
pay packet at the end of the week." There was an almost
rueful note in his voice—one Thane had heard before from
other men who'd left the force for different jobs. Too often,
too, it was the good ones who resigned.

Millan had increased his lead. With ten laps behind him,
he was now beginning to overtake some of the slower cars
which were a lap behind. The field had thinned, more than
one driver pulling off the track with strange metallic noises
coming from his engine.

The track announcer, his voice booming from the scores
of loudspeakers strung round the circuit, interrupted his
commentary to give the information that Millan was now

lapping at one minute twenty-four—a new sports car record for Charterhall.

Beauman was impressed. "Some performance, eh?" He thumbed towards the Ascension pit, where the crew were being noisily jubilant. "They're happy enough!" Then the security man stiffened like a pointer. "Well, that's interesting—someone else I know. Black-and-white-check jacket, matching cap, and a face that the moths have got at. Marked him?"

Thane took a casual glance around. "An old customer?"

"None else. Name of Puggy Carson. He was operating in our manor about three years ago, then headed south for London. Now there he is, large as life, twice as prosperous, and wearing a five-guinea guest badge."

Curiosity aroused, Thane took a second, slower look at the man, standing just on the edge of the Ascension pit space. "He's not on our list. Housebreaker?"

"Nothing so commonplace," murmured Beauman. He let a string of cars howl past, then went on. "Carson was one of the slickest car thieves we ever had. Used to claim there were only two makes he couldn't force in under a minute. One was a Rolls, and the other was one of these foreign doodlebugs."

"Was?"

"Still is, for all I know," said Beauman. "Hey . . . I'm talking like a cop again." His eyes narrowed. "So are you, come to that. Just how much of a pleasure trip is this?"

Thane reached into his inside pocket, found the folded press cutting, and opened it out. The Grand Prix victory group round Erick Millan was poor in detail, like most newspaper pictures. But one of the men standing on the fringe of the photograph had the same rough-edged features. Only a fool would claim it was chance that Puggy Carson seemed so closely interested in the fortunes of the Millan racing stable.

"Dan, do me a favour. Keep one eye on the youngster for five minutes—and the other on Carson. It could be important."

The security man didn't ask questions. He moved a step nearer and boosted the ten-year-old higher on the boundary rail. "Let's see this finish together, young fellow."

There wasn't a police tent within the paddock area. But there was a county car, standing waiting beside the parking area. Thane's warrant card was sufficient introduction.

"Any plain-clothes men this side of the track?" he asked.

The two uniformed men exchanged glances.

"One of the lads might be over at the beer tent," said the driver cautiously. "Taking a bit look about, sir."

"Get him—fast."

The driver doubled off, and it was the radioman's turn.

"I need a message relayed through your County Head-quarters—priority. It's to Inspector Moss, Millside Division, Glasgow . . ."

By the time the first uniformed man returned, followed by a worried, stockily built plain-clothes man who was furtively wiping his lips, the message was going over the air.

Thane returned to his son and Dan Beauman just as the chequered flag swept down to greet Millan's car crossing the finishing line.

"You missed the best bit, Dad—it was terrific." The boy's eyes were bright with excitement.

"Organised?" The security man raised a questioning eye-brow.

"All fixed." Puggy Carson now had a tail in the form of the still anxious Berwickshire officer. In a minute or so Phil Moss would have his message asking for an immediate contact with the English C.R.O. office at Scotland Yard, subject, full details, and record photographs on Carson.

Ending his lap of triumph, Millan brought the sports car

slowly into the pits. As it stopped, he jumped out, pushed his goggles high above the crash hat vizor and, ignoring the rules, took a ready-lighted cigarette from one of the pit crews. Sitting on the pit counter, legs swinging, he watched the rest of the sports cars pull in, steering clear of the first of the big Formula One cars which were already being nosed out to the starting grid.

"Puggy Carson and—him?" Beauman had seen the cutting, and could add a theoretical two and two together. But he was frank in his disbelief.

Thane didn't answer, which in itself was enough for the ex-cop. He made a sympathetic noise. "It's going to be nasty—that's one very popular driver sitting out there."

Out on the track, men with numbered boards stood ready to guide the cars to their proper positions . . . fifteen cars in all, arranged in sandwich layers of three and two according to their practice times. Niccolo's Ferrari was piloted to number one spot by a mechanic, the Italian ace strolling along behind, pulling on his string-backed driving gloves. Number two place was occupied by one of the new Oscas, and the Ascension Special filled the remaining spot on the front row. The shrill note of a siren sounded as the last cars were positioned—one minute to the start. Millan jumped down from the pit counter, ground his cigarette underfoot, and walked across to his car.

"There he is—there's Erick Millan," said Thane's ten-year-old excitedly. "Do you think he'll win again, Dad?"

"He might," agreed Thane reluctantly. "Here—" he fumbled in one pocket. "I got you this on the way back. Don't lose it."

The race programme, open at the Formula One entry list, had its whole page almost covered by the sprawling inked signature "Enrico Niccolo." Even an Italian race star has a considerable respect for the law—especially when the policeman concerned shoves a pen into his hand and practically orders him to supply an autograph.

"Niccolo—" the boy gasped. "He's pretty good too, isn't he?"

"Could be the next world champion, Tom," confirmed Beauman, exchanging an understanding glance with Thane above the boy's head.

"Niccolo . . ." Tom Thane's young loyalties were swinging fast.

Mechanics and marshals had left the track. Now only the starter remained beside the cars. He raised the big Union Jack, swept it down—and in a buffetting, ear-torturing blast of sound the cars were off, all except a lone white Maserati left stranded on the grid, its driver cursing in useless fury. Already the first cars in the race, the Ferrari leading, Millan a close second, and the Osca riding on his tail, were more than halfway round the two-mile course. Their engines bellowed loud and rasping as, one by one, the drivers dropped down a gear, came into the deceptive snake of the Paddock Bend, accelerated again, then were forced to slow for the sharp hairpin of Tofts Turn before the long open straight. The Maserati had been pushed clear to one side—and the three lead cars rocketted past. The first lap was over—but there were another twenty-nine ahead before the Golden Helmet trophy was won.

Thane's attention wasn't on the track. He was watching the Ascension pit, remembering one of the gossip items in Jock Mills's file. Ben MacGhee, it seemed, never watched a big race if he could help it. The car tuned and on the track, the team's head mechanic left any pit-stop work to his assistants. Sheer nervous tension took him away to some corner where he could still hear the tone of his beloved charge but didn't have to endure the duel being fought on the circuit. It wasn't so unusual a trait—no more unusual than the other top tuner who wouldn't even go to a race circuit, but who stayed behind in the home garage, waiting on an end-of-race telephone call.

Four laps passed, and the Osca had dropped back, third place being taken by a green Cooper-Climax, before Mac-Ghee moved. The middle-aged mechanic, head crowned by a broad white sun hat, appeared at the side of the Ascension pit and began to move through the crowd. He passed within inches of where Puggy Carson stood, but the press of fans around was too thick for Thane to see any flicker of recognition pass between them.

"Watch the lad again?" Thane hardly waited for Dan Beauman's answer before he began squeezing in the wake of the engine tuner.

Once clear of the crush, he let MacGhee get ahead and saw him disappear through the entrance of the big refreshment marquee. Thane let three long minutes pass, then followed.

Inside, the marquee was almost deserted. Two waitresses stood behind the rough wooden counter, their only customers two women sitting at a table in the far corner and MacGhee, now nursing a cup of coffee at another table hard against the flapping canvas wall, his back to the entrance. Thane went to the counter, ordered coffee and a sandwich, paid the bill, then took the cup and plate and crossed straight over.

"Mind if I join you?"

MacGhee looked up with a start, coffee slopping from his cup as he half-turned in the chair.

"Sorry if I crept up on you." Thane gave a disarming grin as he took the seat opposite. "Ahh . . . that's better." He stretched his legs with a sigh. "Saw you yesterday, Mr. MacGhee, remember?"

His quarry mumbled acknowledgment.

"Like I said, I've brought my son down for the day," explained Thane cheerfully. "The little devil's nearly walked me off my feet. So I left him with a friend, and sneaked in here for a rest."

The cars whined round again, the noise of their engines seeming to vibrate the thin canvas. MacGhee cocked his head to one side, listening, and then relaxed a fraction.

"Your first time at a race meeting, isn't it?" he asked, lifting the coffee cup slowly and deliberately.

Thane nodded. "The youngster's idea, not mine," he declared. "Though it's exciting enough. A friend had a couple of spare passes, it was Tom's birthday a couple of days ago, and so, well, here we are. Didn't expect to find you here, though. I thought you'd be outside, with your fingers crossed."

MacGhee took a long drink from the cup, ran the sleeve of his white overall across his mouth, and said, "I prefer it here. The technical part, the preparation, that's my excitement." He pursed his lips, listened as the cars tore past again, seemed to wince a trifle as the change-down at the end of the long straight brought a fresh crescendo of noise, and added, "Sometimes racing only means senseless damage to the machine; I'm happier here."

"Pity about Sammy Bell, wasn't it?" said Thane, outwardly casual, choosing every word with care. "From what I can gather he was a pretty good mechanic."

"Bell? Yes, I suppose so." MacGhee kept his eyes on the plain wood of the tabletop.

"Erick Millan felt he might eventually have used Bell on the team—d'you think he'd have been good enough for that?"

"Maybe. He helped out now and again—I'd no complaints."

Thane took a huge bite from the sandwich, chewed busily, let the noise of the cars go past again, then said, "You know, we've got a bit of a problem on our hands about his death."

A distinct quiver began at the tips of the other man's

fingers. He laid one hand flat down on the wood, and clenched the other below the table. "A problem? You mean about—about who killed him."

"That, and other things," admitted Thane. "We'll catch up with the driver eventually, of course. Either that or he'll give himself up. A guilty conscience is a pretty nasty thing to have to live with, you know." He paused: "What's troubling me at the moment is a bit of a minor mystery we've come across. From what we can discover, Bell didn't have many friends, and he wasn't on speaking terms with any family he had. Now we've got a feeling that he may have just left someone—a girl, or a pal perhaps—and was starting off back home when he was killed. Maybe that friend could help, perhaps even saw the car going past before or even after Bell was knocked down."

The cars were coming round again. Thane waited, let sound blast past and die again.

"Know anyone called Jacko?"

The man opposite went suddenly white.

"Jacko, that's the name," said Thane easily. "That's all we've got, a first name."

MacGhee rose from his chair. "Sorry, I can't help. I'd better get back now."

"I'll finish this sandwich," said Thane cheerfully. "And don't worry about that driver—we'll get him."

MacGhee left, almost stumbling against the canvas at the exit.

By the time his father returned, there was no doubting Tom Thane's switch of allegiance. The precious autographed programme clutched tight in one hand, the youngster cheered furiously as Niccolo's Ferrari swept by, a bare thirty yards ahead of Millan's blue-and-red. The Cooper was a much farther distance behind now, the result of a sudden spin at Lodge Corner, the turn at the end of the main straight. Through the loudspeaker system, the commentator's voice was rapidly becoming near-hysterical as he mustered fresh superlatives to describe the duel. Out on the finishing line, the starter was now ready with the yellow Last Lap flag.

One by one, the slower cars in the race whined past. A lamed Lotus, all oil pressure vanished, glided into the pits with a dead engine. Then round the faraway hairpin came the leaders, the commentator now nearly screaming the news that the positions had changed. Millan was ahead— only just, but ahead. It had been the Ferrari's time for trouble, balked while lapping one of the "lame duck" rear guard, a momentary confusion which had allowed his rival to get ahead. It was Niccolo's turn to slipstream, his car tucked hardly a length behind Millan as they stormed past the yellow flag. The Cooper was still third, but it and the other cars were now forgotten in the drama of the battle for first place. The commentator had fallen silent, either exhausted or through wisdom.

Seconds passed and became a minute—then the two bellowing cars reappeared at the far end of the straight, coming down for the last time to where the chequered flag waited.

"It's still Millan," shouted someone. The Ascension Special was in front, the Ferrari still slipstreaming. But even as the news sank home, Niccolo made his move. The Ferrari, with only five hundred yards to go, moved clear and clawed new peak engine revs. Niccolo, his face a tense mask, body crouched low over the steering wheel, seemed to physically force his car past the blue-and-red Ascension. The chequered flag fell as the Ferrari charged across the line, a length and a half in the lead.

One hundred thousand race fans went wild with delight. As Scots, the majority of them had been howling encouragement to Millan as the speed-duel raged before them—but as enthusiasts, they rose to the Italian's last-minute gamble.

The two cars, slowing now, continued round the circuit. Niccolo was showman as much as sportsman. Deliberately idling the red Ferrari, he waved Millan alongside—and the roar of appreciation continued as, side by side, the two cars made a joint lap of honour.

At last, the circuit completed, they turned off the track to enter the paddock area, Niccolo beaming all over his fume-blacked face, one hand upraised in greeting, Millan sitting back a little in his car, acknowledgments fewer, emotions cloaked behind a somewhat strained air of good fellowship. The cars halted, and were surrounded by a minor wave of pressmen. Shutters clicked, a scattering of cine-cameras whined, while the two men posed side by side. A procession of race officials appeared on the fringe of the crush, pushing their way through with the winner's spoils—the Gold Helmet trophy and the accompanying thousand-pound cheque, the latter discreetly concealed in a plain white envelope.

"Let's skip the presentation, youngster," decided Thane. "Time we called it a day. The longer we leave it, the worse the traffic is going to be on the road home."

Already the crowd was beginning to thin. There was still another item, a scratch handicap event, waiting to be run before the programme was completed. But the wiser spectators were already filtering towards the car parks and the homeward journey. Like them, Thane had no wish to be involved in the inevitable series of traffic tangles bound to occur when the full volume of the crowd began to surge out on to the few narrow roads which led from the circuit exits.

His son gave a sigh of complete small-boy satisfaction. "All right. But, Dad, can I take the programme to school tomorrow? Please? Then I can show them I've really got Niccolo's autograph."

"After that performance, I wouldn't mind having his autograph myself, youngster," said Dan Beauman. The security man used a large handkerchief to wipe the perspiration from his forehead, and gave the boy a broad wink. "Now I've got to go and see nobody tries to run away with all the money. Colin—" his voice grew more serious. "It's been good seeing you again. And whatever you're up to, good luck. I don't suppose I can really help in it, but you know how to get hold of me. If Puggy Carson's mixed up in anything you can be sure there's crooked money in the background."

They shook hands.

"And Colin—" there was a hint of embarrassment in Beauman's final farewell. "I'm glad it worked out."

Minutes later, his car the last but one to escape across the track from the paddock before the tarmac exits were sealed for the last race, Thane silently echoed the security man's sentiments.

A small boy's idols, once created, can't be lightly interfered with. He cursed himself for a fool for not realising until nearly too late that if the boy was to be left with one lasting memory of their day out together that memory would more than likely be the thrill of seeing Erick Millan in action. Until that realisation, bringing Tom along to the circuit had seemed an ideal way of giving the boy a birthday outing which at the same time would serve the more important purpose of providing Thane with what, to an outsider, would have appeared the most natural reason in the world for turning up at the race meeting. Well, the camouflage had succeeded. The information on Puggy Carson, his refreshment tent interview with Ben MacGhee, both these things were valuable dividends.

But he blessed that swarthy, sun-bronzed Italian who'd steered the Ferrari to victory. The race driver, now probably drinking a champagne toast to his own success, had saved Thane's day. The burly detective had come close to falling into a parental trap of his own making. He assured himself it wouldn't happen again.

"Dad—" an anxious nudge from his young passenger snapped Thane back to reality. He braked their car inches short of an irate traffic policeman whose white-gloved hand was raised in an equally irate signal to halt. Behind the car, other traffic jerked to a standstill.

The constable stalked round, and his face peered in through the driver's window. "What do you think you're up to, eh, Mac?" he rumbled. "Think I'm holding up my hand for the fun of it, eh?"

Thane mumbled an apology. "Sorry, officer, I was daydreaming."

"Daydreaming." The constable sniffed. "Aye, I've heard that before. You see these characters racing back there, then you get into your wee car and start thinking about how you could do the same. That your son?"

"Yes." Thane was suitably humble.

"At that rate, you're old enough to know better." The Borderer's fingers strayed towards his tunic pocket and his notebook. Then he changed his mind. "Ach, on you go— you're holding up the traffic. Here, lad, you look bright enough. Keep an eye on him." He stood back, and waved them on.

Thane grated the car into gear and drove off, awaiting the inevitable.

"Dad—"

"Uh-huh."

"Your face has gone red," said his son innocently. "Why didn't you tell him you were a policeman too?"

"There's some chocolate in the dash pocket," said Thane shortly. "Take it and be quiet."

It was nearly eight P.M. by the time they got home, to find Phil Moss occupying Thane's favourite chair while Mary Thane prepared a king-sized omelette for the evening meal.

Afterwards, with Tom and his sister in their beds asleep and Mary washing up, Moss relaxed with a sigh of satisfaction.

"Well, you didn't waste your time down there," he agreed. "The Yard have come through with Carson's record. He's all your pal Beauman said he was."

"Pictures?"

"Coming up on the night plane from London," said Moss. "Messenger's collecting them on arrival, and copies are going out to the men watching Menran's place—there's been no movement there all day, incidentally.

"Then, of course, we had a pretty negative report from Berwickshire. Carson was tailed till he left the circuit. He made no attempt to speak to any of the Ascension pit team, and didn't try to approach Erick Millan—though he'd have had a hard job doing it. Seems Millan was practically mobbed by fans for the rest of the race meeting."

Thane yawned and stretched. "You know, Phil, if there's a weak link in this outfit I think I've got it spotted. . . . Ben MacGhee. He practically jumped out of his skin when I asked him about Jacko. Hey, what happened with the delectable Ida Murdock?"

Moss squirmed. "She's fixed it for next Sunday. Unless," he added gloomily, "she 'just happens' to see me before then. What do you do with that kind of woman?"

"Take to the hills," advised Thane. "Here, throw me over that paper. Let's see if there's anything worth while on the telly."

His companion brightened.

CHAPTER FIVE

After most race meetings there is, inevitably, a celebrity dinner. If some of the drivers present occasionally display more of a thirst than an appetite, well, nobody worries too much. If the resultant aftermath of the occasion includes minor exuberances such as throwing a friend's bed and mattress bodily out of a hotel window, heaving blonde young ladies into the nearest duckpond, or attempting to commandeer the local refuse wagon, again, allowances are made.

Bills for damage have a habit of being settled without query. Blonde young ladies are usually wise enough to know that only popular girls end up in duckponds. And the wise among the older onlookers watch it all, make sure things don't get too much out of hand, and call the whole performance "restoring the balance." When a man has put yet another race behind him and discovers he's still in one piece then the tension is off. The dry-mouthed apprehension, the taut bow-string nervousness which must be hidden, all the things which can make a man vomit while he waits, have gone. He celebrates.

Enrico Niccolo was, naturally, guest of honour at the Golden Helmet banquet. The trophy before him as a proud centrepiece, he was flanked at the top table on one side by the president of the race committee and on the other by a visiting film starlet who happened to have a shrewd publicity agent.

Erick Millan was also at the top table, his place a few chairs removed from the central limelight which had come so near to being his own. The meal concluded, the race president rose, to launch into a short speech about Niccolo, not one word of which the Italian understood.

"*Grazie . . . mi permette. . . .*" in turn, almost unrecognisable in dinner jacket and black tie, Niccolo replied with a few sentences in machine-gun Italian.

When it was over, Millan escaped. He dodged a young Lotus driver armed with a soda syphon, murmured regrets to three gentlemen from London who had plans involving the hotel flagpole and some mysteriously acquired articles of underwear. His overnight grip was ready packed, the hotel bill squared, and his car waiting.

As usual, the Sprite two-seater fired to life at the first turn of the starter motor. Millan slammed the car into gear, booted the accelerator, and concentrated on the drive back to Glasgow.

He reached the city about eleven, steered through the quiet, Sunday-hushed streets, and finally halted the car outside the block of flats which was home. There had been a time, a long time, when Millan lived with his uncle. But it was two years now since he'd ended that arrangement to their unspoken but mutual relief.

Inside, the elevator took him up the three floors. Its gate purred open, closed behind him again, and he strode the short distance along the hallway, key in hand.

But at the first grate of his key in the lock, the door was opened from within.

The girl stood there, her eyes sparkling, the shaded wall-lights of the room beyond catching the burnished high-lights of her long, copper-hued hair.

"I've been waiting," she pouted.

He shut the door, tossed the grip on to a handy chair, and kissed her, hard and exploratory. Finally, she squirmed from his grasp. "Don't be in such a rush, Erick. The race is over." She smoothed the silk of her dress, moved across to the bottle-laden cabinet, and asked over one shoulder, "Drink?"

"Scotch, straight."

"I've been here nearly an hour." She finished pouring. Millan had sunk down into an armchair, and he gained pleasure from just watching her come over, glasses in hand.

"You knew about the dinner. I said about eleven when I gave you the key. Here—"

Obediently, she perched on the arm beside him and sipped her glass. "Glad I waited?"

The telephone began ringing before he could answer.

The girl stamped one neatly clad foot on the thick-piled carpet. "Not again—that's the fourth time since I arrived."

The shrill ringing beat continued. "Who was it?" Millan got up, glass still in hand, and crossed over.

"Darling—" she sounded almost shocked. "I don't take other people's calls. It could be embarrassing. . . ."

He waved her to silence, and lifted the receiver.

The voice at the other end of the line was hoarse with relief. "Millan? It's Liscomb here— I've been trying to get you all evening."

"I'm just back. What's up?" A faint smile on his face, Millan watched the redhead curl into a more comfortable position on the chair arm.

"Your uncle's been prowling around!" The showroom manager didn't try to conceal his agitation. "Turned up this afternoon, took a sniff around the cars, and quizzed one of the salesmen."

The girl forgotten, Millan tensed. "You're sure it was Old Ludd?"

"'Course I'm sure," Liscomb's voice came back along the

line. "I know what he looks like, even if he doesn't know me."

"What did he ask?"

Liscomb sounded puzzled. "That's just it. He pokes around the cars, asks about prices, how long we've been open, that sort of thing. Then he wants to know who runs the place, and the salesman tells him I do."

"And then?"

"He prowls around a bit more, then shoves off. What's it all about—is he on to us?"

"I'll call you back." Millan put down the receiver, cutting short the other man's protests.

"I've got to go out," he told the girl.

"But Erick . . ." indignation mixed with sudden anger and disappointment. "Not right away, surely. I've been waiting . . ."

"This can't." He kissed her on the lips with detached precision. "Be a good girl and just leave when you're ready. This may take time."

Open-mouthed, she watched him go, saw the door slam behind him, then heard the whine of the elevator.

"Damn. Oh, the lousy—"

The rest of her comments would have come as a distinct shock to her ever-loving parents. Slowly, she went through to the bedroom to collect her coat.

The Ascension garage closed at nine on Sunday evenings, but lights still burned within when Millan's car slid to a halt at the kerb. He gave a grunt of satisfaction, unlocked the small private door set to one side of the main, closed entry gate, and went on in, his feet echoing as he crossed the concrete floor.

The lights came from the faraway section of the workshop area. Ben MacGhee had travelled back to the city from Charterhall with the rest of the pit team, crammed into the transporter with its two-car load. The others had gone home. But MacGhee, as usual, had stayed behind for a slow, methodical check of his charges. The engine cover was removed from the eight-cylinder G.P. car, and the harsh glare of an inspection lamp burned above as he contemplated the partly dismantled fuel injection unit. He looked up at the sound of footsteps, and waited, one hand stroking the metal of the engine block.

"Well?" There was no need for Millan to expand on his query.

"Injectors again." MacGhee gestured towards the bench, where the rest of the unit lay in bits. "I warned you they were a wee fraction out. More testing time, that's what we need. If I'd had that, you'd have been able to keep ahead of that dam' Ferrari ice-cream wagon. Mind you, she went well enough—"

"We lost." Millan cut him short with savage emphasis. "That's all that counts out there. It's not one of your blasted test beds. You win or you lose, and if you lose then the rest doesn't matter."

"The crowd didn't think so," protested the mechanic. "Not after the way you drove. You'd bad luck, that's all. Wait till the new engines are ready and things will be different."

"You've said that before," growled Millan. But, obviously mollified, he turned to the real subject on his mind. "Any sign of Old Ludd while you've been here?"

"Your uncle—no, I've been on my own since the lads shoved off," said MacGhee. "Why?"

"I'll be back." Millan clattered up the iron stairway to the office level above, passed his uncle's room, dark and un-occupied, and entered his own office, next door. He switched on the light, crossed to his desk, and checked the drawers. They were still locked—that was something, at any rate. He held the only key. Unless—his eyes narrowed, and he turned towards the nearest of the two filing cabinets. It had three drawers, the top for correspondence in his post as Ascension's sales director, the middle devoted to inter-office memoes and advertising records, and the bottom marked plainly "Mr. E. Millan—Personal."

He pulled it open. Inside, the cardboard folders, carefully labelled, were fat with letters and documents devoted to the Ascension racing team's activities. The rear folder's bulk was reassuring, but he took it out, and inspected the contents. They seemed intact. Nothing which linked him with Bacarro Motors and Liscomb was left lying about—but a shrewd mind, inspecting the rear folder, with its detailed financial calculations, its invoices and accounts, all devoted to the two racing cars below, could have come to some swift conclusions as to the amount of money draining into their preparation and their racing programme. Maybe Old Ludd had been looking them over—but how did that link with his turning up at the showroom that afternoon?

Carefully, item by item, he went through the file again. Slowly, he realised that though nothing was missing there was no doubt someone had been there before him. Erick Millan had close to a passion for correct filing—and the odd letter out of chronological order, two receipted bills side by side instead of widely separated, told their own story.

So his uncle had been snooping. But that still didn't account for his sudden arrival at the car showroom, a place he should know nothing about. Liscomb was right. Old Ludd's arrival and the disarranged file were too much of coincidence to be true.

Millan left his own room, stopped outside the next-door office, and tried the handle. It was locked. Grim-faced, he went back down the stairway. A crumpled cigarette in one corner of his mouth, Ben MacGhee was still there, the injector unit spread out on the bench before him.

"Still at it?"

The mechanic let tobacco smoke drift from his nostrils, and nodded. "I think I've got the answer," he said with quiet satisfaction. "I'll get some time on it tomorrow. . . ."

"Maybe not." Millan played the other man with cold calculation.

MacGhee blinked. "What d'you mean? It's simple enough. . . ."

"Old Ludd's been poking around," said Millan with icy emphasis. "He's been through my stuff upstairs, and Liscomb discovered him quizzing his way around the showroom this afternoon."

MacGhee paled, one hand reaching out to draw assurance from the metal parts beside him. "How—" he took the cigarette from his mouth and moistened his lips. "Is he on to us? How did he know about it?"

Millan shook his head. "It's too early yet to panic. The files are one thing—he's going to have me over a barrel tomorrow when he comes up with this idea of taking over the team as part of the business." He gave a harsh laugh. "It would have been worth seeing his face when he saw some of the costs. But the showroom—it could just have been chance. He's got a habit of going around on his own at the week end. It's not impossible he was just passing and looked in to see how the stock was priced. He's been grilling me about Ascension's sales."

"But you don't believe it, do you?" MacGhee refused to accept the convenient solution. "What'll he do?"

"Do?" Millan's whole manner changed to that of a fighter in a common cause. "He probably doesn't know enough to do anything—yet. And we're too close to what we want now. Too close to let anybody stop us. How soon do you reckon the first new engine will be ready?"

"A month." MacGhee was almost tearful. "But if we're caught, we're finished. I've got a family, Mr. Millan."

"So?" Millan went over to where the two precious castings lay covered in dust sheets. "It's all here, Ben." He exerted all of his silky persuasion. "We'll soon be on our way up that championship table—I'll find my own way to the top without any team manager deciding who does what, which driver is to have the best car, who gets the chances and who simply acts as pacemaker. And it'll be with your engines, Ben—your big chance to show the smart boys at the factories."

MacGhee only half-rose to the bait. "If your uncle knows . . ."

"Then we'll need to do something about it, that's all," said Millan softly. "If Old Ludd makes trouble, he'll have to be stopped, one way—or another."

It took a moment or two to sink in. Then: "We can't—"

"Accidents happen," breathed Millan. "Sammy Bell could tell you that. I'll know tomorrow morning. And I'll tell you then, Ben."

His companion blinked, then shook his head. "Not me. Not that."

"You'll do what's needed." Millan's words hit home. "You're in this, Ben, just the same as the rest of us."

The other man flushed. "Not if it means like Bell—not murder."

"Who said murder?" Millan raised an eyebrow. "Poor Sammy had an accident—ask the police. But then, Sammy wouldn't do as he was told either, would he?" There was no attempt to disguise the menace in his tone. "If you want to keep your shiny bright engines, then you're going to have to do just what I decide. At this moment we're sitting so pretty it's almost laughable. Carson, Liscomb, Menran— they're professionals. We're the amateurs, but the amateurs who've made it all possible. I'm not letting Old Ludd stand in my way."

MacGhee dragged his cigarettes from the top pocket of his overalls, and lit one from the smouldering butt of the previous. "You say don't worry—but what about the police?"

"Thane?" Millan shrugged. "He came along to the track to gape, like all the other peasants. His kid was with him. Thane's just a local C.I.D. brass who's got a hit-and-run case on his hands. Sure, the police are bound to be having blood pressure at the number of cars being knocked off. But it's their Headquarters people who're worrying over that—I know."

MacGhee twirled the fresh cigarette between his oil-stained fingers. "Thane bumped into me in the tea tent. He wanted to know if I'd ever heard Bell mention a pal called Jacko!"

The news didn't budge Millan's assessment. "He's harmless. I'm getting sick trying to thump that into your head." He turned to leave. A moment later, the outer door shut behind him.

With a strange sound close to a sob, MacGhee gathered together the scattered portions of equipment before him. No more that night—he switched off the inspection lamp, and headed out to his own car. For MacGhee, home had suddenly become a refuge.

Erick Millan was back at the Ascension garage at nine the next morning. It was a dull, grey, typically Scottish Monday, the sort of day when workers drag their feet while typists, their head rough-combed, find shorthand difficult and concentration almost impossible. But for Millan, waiting in his room while the minutes dragged past, it was a time of tension.

At last, dead on nine-thirty, he heard a door opening, sounds of activity in the next room, and then the desk intercom beeped. He flipped the switch.

"Erick . . . come through, will you?"

He got up, walked the few paces along the corridor, knocked, and entered the other office.

"Sit down." Stiff and upright behind his desk, Old Ludd's voice was carefully neutral. "Cigarette?" He lifted the lid of the wooden box.

"No thanks." Millan was busy trying to sum up the other man's attitude. There was a strange refusal to meet his gaze, an air close to reluctance hanging over Old Ludd, damping his usual grumbling, straight-to-the-point manner.

Ludd Millan closed the box, fiddled with the still unopened mail before him, and chewed slowly on his lower lip.

"We were to talk about your racing budget," he said finally. "But it's a waste of time, isn't it?"

"I don't follow—it was your idea, Uncle, not mine," said Millan coolly.

Old Ludd growled low in his throat. "For the first time in my life, Erick, I'm sitting here not knowing what to do or what to say. I was here yesterday afternoon, trying to—trying to see just how high a committment the firm could stand. I wanted some facts to help me—facts that would let me offer you a package deal." He stopped, one hand running wearily over the close-cropped iron-grey hair. "I went into your room to try to find these facts. . . ."

"I know." Millan changed his mind, reached forward, took a cigarette from the box, and lit it. "I knew somebody had been at the budget file. Find what you wanted?"

The older man restrained himself by a major effort. "Where's it all come from, Erick? Don't try to fool me, now . . . no talk of advertising contracts or prize money. You couldn't borrow that much money, even if you tried."

"That's true enough," agreed Millan. "Racing drivers seem to be rated a poor risk. Their future's—uncertain." He leaned forward on the desk, chin in one hand. "Supposing I just say it's my business?"

Old Ludd slammed the wood with pounding force. "Damn you, Erick, you're my brother's only son. Otherwise

I'd have heaved you straight out on to the street. I'll give you a last chance. What's your connection with this ragtag outfit Bacarro Motors?"

"I'm not sure what you're getting at," parried Millan.

His uncle snorted. "Don't try it on me, Erick. You may be a second-rate tin god to the racing fans, but from where I'm sitting you're nothing more than a crooked little swine. Are you going to tell me?"

"You've got me on the money side," agreed Millan carelessly. "But the rest of it—Bacarro Motors—who says I even know the place?"

"Don't you know?" said the older man. "Then that's something for you to worry about, isn't it? Get out, Erick. You can come to see me when you decide to tell the rest of it. I'll be here."

Millan rose, ground out his cigarette on the big glass ash tray. "Don't wait too long," he advised, then, a final sneer, "Keep an eye on the petty cash while you're at it."

The door slammed shut. With clumsy, almost savage deliberation, Ludd Millan forced his attention to the unopened letters on his desk.

"As long as you keep behind the curtain, sir, you're all right." The fair-haired young Marine Division man emphasised his point with a cautionary hand as Thane bent behind the tripod-mounted binoculars. The Chief Inspector peered through the eyepieces, corrected the focus on one lens to a fraction more power, and found himself apparently only a few feet away from the entrance to the wooden garage below. Straightening up, he edged clear.

"Seems you've got yourselves nicely settled," he told the two plain-clothes men. A chair was placed handily beside the tripod-mounted glasses. Another armchair had been dragged into the small bedroom, and an electric kettle lay close beside a wall plug. Overnight, a telephone had been installed in one corner, a temporary lead arranged by a co-operative Post Office official.

The fair-haired cop grinned. "Householder's being help-ful, sir," he confirmed. "She and her husband normally sleep here, but they've moved into the front room."

"How about neighbours?" The binoculars had been cleverly mounted, their lenses concealed from ground level by the sweep of curtain fabric.

"No troubles there, sir," said the second plain-clothes man. "Mrs. Munro's told them we're pals of her son. He's in the army—we're supposed to be here on a spot of leave."

"Good cover," said Thane approvingly. "You've got that picture of Carson, and you know what to do—right?"

The men nodded. Thane was their second visitor that morning. The other had been a d.c. from the Scientific Branch who'd waited until he'd managed to take a quick camera-shot of Jacko Menran arriving to start work. The camera had been interesting—one of these automatic German models which took three pictures in a two-second interval. But having a Chief Inspector breathing down your neck was a different matter, especially when he came from an-other division and they were uncertain how to handle him.

Thane knew the signs. "I'll get going," he told them. "Where's Mrs. Munro? I'd like a word with her."

"Probably in the kitchen, sir—I'll see," volunteered one of the men.

"I'll manage. Keep in touch." He went out into the narrow hallway and, guided by the clatter of dishes, found the housewife busy by the sink.

Mrs. Munro, small, tidily dressed beneath a large floral apron, put down the plate she'd been drying. She was about fifty, her dark hair in a tight bun at the nape of her neck.

"My name's Thane," he introduced himself. "I'm the

cause of this invasion. I just wanted to thank you for letting us use your home."

"Don't worry yourself about that," she reassured him. "We're happy enough to help. It's good company for me during the day, anyway."

Thane noticed the small mountain of ready-peeled potatoes on the kitchen table. "Your family gets home for lunch?"

She twinkled. "There's just me and my man—oh, and the lad of course, he's away. But all you polis have big appetites."

"You don't have to feed them you know," Thane told her, surprised.

"Ach, they told me that yesterday," she nodded. "Them with their wee bit pieces. I just told them nobody's staying here under my roof and no' getting a square meal."

There was, he decided, no cause for further concern over the Peaceview Terrace stake-out.

Back at Millside, Phil Moss was waiting.

"D.C. Beech is beginning to haunt me," he declared as Thane settled behind his desk. "Does the name Putter mean anything to you?"

Thane blinked. "No—should it?"

"That," said Moss wearily, "is exactly what I'm trying to find out. Mr. Putter phoned this morning—phoned while I was still trying to get my coat off. It seems he had a conversation with our D.C. Beech last Friday, and young Beech shovelled him off to see a lawyer."

"Wait a minute—I remember now," mused Thane. "Beech did have a couple of items uncleared when he went off. He left the details, and both sounded crank-type."

"Huh. Well, crank or no crank, Mr. Putter's coming round this afternoon," said Moss. "Beech may have shovelled him on to a solicitor—but the solicitor's shovelled him straight back on to us."

"Putter—is he the one who's being death-rayed or the one who's going to sue?" Thane raked through the small mountain of material on his desk tray.

"The one who's going to sue." Moss gave a reminiscent shudder. "From the way he talked, he's likely to end up trying to have us fired into the bargain."

Thane found the cardboard folder that Beech had left. "Here we are . . . well, if friend Putter's coming round, we'd better have a senior officer to see him this time, eh?" He flipped the folder across the desk. "It's all yours, Inspector."

"Me?" Moss accepted the task with little grace. "All right, but I tell you, Beech is haunting me."

Apart from Mr. Putter's phone call, Moss had little to report. Jock Mills was still working on his special assignment—the *Bugle* crime reporter hoped to deliver the result sometime in the afternoon. The Dolman gang had gone through the Sheriff Court that morning, remanded in custody "for further inquiry" on a three-pronged charge-sheet of housebreaking, attempted safeblowing, and being found in possession of explosives.

"Oh, and Sergeant MacLeod's still tracing wrecked cars and registration books," said Moss as an afterthought. "He wants to know if he's to keep at it."

"Yes, he may as well," agreed Thane. "It's a pretty slim chance, but we've got to check it out."

Picking up the "crank" file, Moss left to pass on the Millside chief's verdict.

Thane lifted the telephone. "Superintendent Laurence at Headquarters, please, Joyce," he told the switchboard girl, whistling tunelessly through his teeth while he waited on the connection.

"Now I wouldn't know what you'd be after," the Scientific Branch boss's voice finally boomed along the line. "Well, I'm ready."

"What's the verdict?" probed Thane cautiously.

"Pretty good," declared Laurence. "Not conclusive, of course, but pretty good all the same. The grit samples from Bell's shoes match with the stuff we got from your bloke's number nines . . . you know that already. We've finished checking on the shell sand, thanks to one of my lads working through the firm's order books since almost dawn. There are only about half a dozen places in the city where ready-mixed concrete containing that sand has been poured for a garage floor—most of their work's building structure foundations. Ascension's one of the garages. Now leave me alone, will you? I'm busy."

"Thanks, Dan." Thane replaced the receiver. He got up, went over to the window, and looked down into the yard below. Wearing gumboots, a uniformed constable was busy washing down one of the divisional cars. Thane glanced at his watch, wondered if he should phone Buddha Ilford, remembered the proverb advising "Never trouble trouble till trouble troubles you," and was still trying to make up his mind when the office door crashed open.

Phil Moss burst into the room, and thumped D.C. Beech's crank file down on the desk. "That young idiot! Colin, do you know what Putter's complaint is about? Here we've been chasing our tails, and there's a thing like this lying waiting under our noses—"

"Steady on, Phil," protested Thane. "What's happened?"

Spluttering, Moss pointed to the file. "That—look, Putter came round to complain about his car. Maybe he had things mixed up and told it like a Chinese puzzle—in fact, he wanted us to have a go at the manufacturers. But listen to this—Beech's summary of their interview." He pulled the file towards him again, took out the top sheet of close-typed paper. "Just listen.

"'Complainer is the owner of a six-month-old saloon car, registration number 641 WGG. Reports that following recent accident had occasion to acquire new mechanical parts with a view to carrying out home repairs. On attempting to fit these parts, ascertained that two were of wrong size and fitting, though ordered for correct engine series. Produces correspondence with manufacturers in which they confirm that quoted engine number 6–47X2–7 is of the type for which correct spare parts were supplied. Complainer, who purchased the car 641 WGG secondhand a few weeks ago, claims that it is in fact fitted with an older model engine bearing an incorrect serial number, adds that he as a result holds goods bearing a fraudulent factory description, and requests police proceedings. Have advised complainer that the matter does not appear one for police investigation, and that he should consult his solicitor with a view to possible civil action.'"

"Let me see that." Thane took the report sheet, read it through, and grimaced. "Well, at least young Beech got the facts. Stolen car?"

"What else?" Moss prowled the room, trying hard to temper his indignation. "Beech is usually thorough enough —can't understand it. Though these twins arriving have had him in the clouds for days, I suppose; and he hasn't been involved in any of the car inquiries. Still—if that engine number matches with the one listed in the registration book there's only one answer. A faked engine number and faked book, both needed because the car's 'hot,' one of the ones we've been looking for."

To Thane, it seemed the only logical answer. If they were lucky—he fought hard against the temptation to premature enthusiasm. "All right, Phil, we won't wait until Putter turns up here this afternoon. Get out to him, find if his story stands up, where he bought the car and who owned it before him. Once we've got that, we can start checking on any car of that description that's been stolen— and have a close look at the engine number." The phone on his desk began ringing. He picked up the receiver: "Thane."

Impatient to go, Moss waited by the door.

"Hold on." The chief looked across. "It's our lucky day, Phil. Puggy Carson's just driven up to Menran's place. Get moving—I'll take care of this end."

With an exuberant thumbs-up sign, the thin figure vanished. Thane turned back to the phone: "Right, now give me it again."

At the other end of the line, the Marine plain-clothes man, eyes still glued to the binocular lenses, spoke quietly, keeping his facts crisp. "I'm watching the garage right now, sir. The car arrived about two minutes ago—light blue Austin, registration 240 CHZ. It stopped just short of the doors, and Carson got out."

"You're sure it's Carson?"

"Positive, sir. My mate double-checked. Carson knocked on the doors, Menran came out, and the car's just been driven in. They're shutting the doors now." He had a last glimpse of Menran, then the doors swung together, blotting the garage interior from view. "That's it so far, sir. Instructions?"

"Just sit tight," ordered Thane. "If Carson leaves, let him—it's the car we're interested in. Any other vehicles in that garage?"

"None, sir."

"Good. If and when that Austin comes out again it may look very different from what it is now. We'll have an observation van standing by ready to pick it up—so the moment it shows its nose outside again we'll need a full description to radio control. They'll pass the word."

"Will do, sir."

A poker player would probably have described the situation as being on parallel with having a run of indifferent cards, then suddenly being presented with what could be the makings of a royal flush—with the sneaking feeling that

the vital picture cards were lying waiting at the top of the
dealer's pack.

The hand was shaping, and now it was up to Thane to
play for the jackpot. That was how it went—you plugged
away at a case, making crawling progress, and then the
planned, plotted, sometimes infinitely slow moves paid off
with an accompanying bonus. As the line from Peaceview
Terrace went dead, he pinged the receiver rest.

"Yes, sir?" Joyce had learned to keep a priority watch
on the Chief Inspector's extension.

"Headquarters control, Joyce—and some tea!" Bless you,
D.C. Beech, patiently listening to little men with long-
winded complaints, then turning their moans into weary,
factual report sheets—even if you didn't have the chance
to realise the significance of a man called Putter. And the
two men with their binoculars, who knew that whatever
happened, their role was static, that someone else from
another division was going to harvest the fruits.

"Control on the line, sir." The switchboard girl completed
the connection.

The duty inspector in the Headquarters radio room
listened as Thane spoke, scribbled on a message form, and
had the sheet whisked across to the control operator.

"Observation van's being called now," he confirmed
laconically. Over the telephone wire, Thane could hear the
message already going out over the short-wave system.

"Now the car . . ."

"I've got the list here, Chief Inspector," said the headquarters officer. "Registration number 240 CHZ—no, no report in yet. If it's been flogged, the owner probably doesn't
know about it."

"If it comes in, don't circulate it," warned Thane. "Chief
Superintendent Ilford's authority."

"Yours is enough," murmured the other man dryly. "I
see your point—no sense some car crew remembering they

saw it, and spoiling your setup. What about tracing the owner?"

"We'll do that at this end," said Thane.

He hung up, pressed the desk buzzer, and in double-quick time a detective constable entered. The main office grapevine knew when things were starting to hum—and the Millside C.I.D. squad were eager for action.

"This one's yours, Brookfield. Get on to Motor Taxation, find the owner of a car 240 CHZ, light blue Austin, get out after him, and ask him where it is right now. When he finds it's gone, check back. But don't tell him we know where it is—just say it was seen being driven by a suspicious character. If that Austin gets mucked around before we get it back, I don't want us landed with a bill for damages. Sergeant MacLeod out there?"

"Yes sir."

"Right—send him in."

Brookfield left, and Thane ticked off another item on his mental list.

"Want me, sir?" A weary-looking MacLeod stood in the doorway, a sheaf of papers in one hand. "I've got the wrecked car sheets here—"

"Toss them in the bucket," ordered Thane.

"But Inspector Moss said—"

"Forget them. We're moving now, sergeant. I want a search warrant for Menran Auto Electrics—suspected stolen property. Then I want another one for Ascension Garages' head office—suspected murder weapon." He gave a grim smile of anticipation.

Mr. Francis Putter, a paunchy fifteen-stone individual with beery breath and a clerical grey suit obviously overdue a trip to the cleaners, owned a small photographic shop in Fisk Street, close to the fringe of the Millside divisional area. He turned over charge of the shop counter to his sole assistant, a pimply-faced teen-ager, and ushered Moss through to the little office at the rear of his premises.

"I've got all the papers here," he wheezed noisily. "It's about time you fellows got around to doing something about it—the amount of taxes I've got to pay on this business, even with a pretty well shoe-string profit, I'm entitled to expect some action. You can take notes while I tell you about it."

"Maybe it would be better if I asked the questions," said Moss with unaccustomed politeness. "Purely to save your time." For the moment, Mr. Putter was too vital a factor to be upset by the detective's instinctive desire to retort in kind.

"Easier for me to tell it," said Putter, giving a petulant scowl. "But all right—let's get on with it." He moved a pile of cardboard boxes from the solitary chair, then, breathing heavily, sat down.

"First of all, you bought the car how long ago?"

"About two months ago—you've got all this already."

"Just making sure, Mr. Putter," said Moss gently. "Where did you buy it?"

"Bacarro Motors in Kempville Street—they're a fairly new firm, but they keep their prices reasonable, and I've got one or two friends who've dealt with them. No complaint there, Inspector. It's the makers I'm after, and I know what I'm talking about. Nine months ago they changed over the engine design on this model, put in a new unit with a bit more pep in it—and easier on the old m.p.g. Factory's probably had one or two of the old engines still lying around, and they've stuck one in my car and thought they could get away with it." He wheezed vociferously. "But I'm nobody's fool, Inspector. I'm a businessman, and to be that today you've got to keep your wits about you."

"Could I see the registration book?"

After a few minutes' search, Putter located the pasteboard document, buried deep in his inside pocket. He handed it over along with a bulky, once-white envelope. "There's the rest of your evidence. Receipt for cash sale— always pay cash—copy of the letter I sent to the makers, the one they had the damned nerve to write back to me, and a list of the parts I bought, then found were useless."

"I'd like to hold on to these for a day or so." Moss stroked his nose gently. "Tell me about the accident, Mr. Putter."

The heavy breathing increased in tempo. "Blame an idiot of a bus driver. He saw some woman waiting by a crossing, pulled up sharp, and didn't give me a chance. The car ran straight into the back of the bus—bodywork damage, radiator smashed, and the engine messed about. A hundred and fifty pounds' worth of damage, and to add insult to injury the police patrol who finally arrived on the scene charged me with careless driving."

"Well . . ." Moss stifled a smile. "That's not my department, Mr. Putter. You decided to repair the engine yourself—couldn't the insurance company do that?"

Putter wriggled uncomfortably. "Ah well, they are, in a way. The car's being repaired at a garage belonging to a friend of mine. He's doing the bodywork and that sort of thing. We've—well, we've come to an arrangement about the mechanical side. I was a mechanic in the army—that's where I got this bronchitis, and no pension either. Anyway, I'm doing the engine up and . . ."

"And he charges the insurance company for the full job, then you split the difference." Moss turned a glare of thin-faced disapproval towards the embarrassed motorist. "Well, that's your business, Mr. Putter. Just one more point. Have you ever mentioned this trouble about the engine to the people you bought the car from?"

"No, it's nothing to do with them."

Moss put away his notebook. "We'll look into it, Mr.

Putter. But for a start, we'll need to move your car down to the police garage for a full examination. It may take a day or so. Any objection?"

Putter shook his head. "Keep it as long as you like," he wheezed. "I'm suing the bus company for loss of use. The garage is just down the road—you can't miss it."

For Moss, the next hour was a time of little rest. First, he located Putter's car, its damaged bodywork smoothed and beaten back into shape but still only covered in rough primer paint. A brief interview with the garage owner, a phone call back to Headquarters, and he'd organised the vehicle's removal. After that, there was a brief car journey which still left him with considerable satisfaction, then some further mileage which ended as the C.I.D. car drew in at the city's police garage in Helen Street.

The garage, a big red brick building with petrol pumps, wash bays, its own fully equipped workshop and all the other facilities needed to keep force's transport fleet, from patrol vans to motor scooters, in constant trim, could hardly be called a piece of architectural beauty. Its background, too, an interesting view of the Govan area garbage incinerator, had little to appeal to the artistic eye. But it was functional, highly functional, and all the equipment needed by the group of men gathered within was ready and to hand.

They greeted him briefly—Thane, Dan Laurence, and one of his squad from the Bureau, Superintendent Beam from the Traffic Department, who'd come over for the pure purpose of keeping an eye on what the other firms were up to within the precincts of the mobile section, and, most surprising of all, Chief Detective Superintendent Ilford.

When the city's C.I.D. boss put in an appearance it was a sure sign that action was due—major action which would first require his tacit assent. Buddha Ilford didn't generally get in the way of his divisional officers, but there were times when he demanded the final say in their plans, plans which, once approved, he'd back to the last ditch whether they succeeded or failed.

"Ready, gentlemen? This way then, please." Superintendent Beam acted as guide, and the party threaded after him in strict order of seniority. Through the building, out a rear door and across the back yard they went to a covered-in area where Mr. Putter's car lay waiting, towed in half an hour previous by a breakdown truck. The police sergeant-mechanic who stiffened as they approached had already been at work. The car's bonnet was dismantled, distributor and other auxiliaries moved clear, and one side of the engine block polished clear of oil and soot until it gleamed in the dull light.

"Your party, Thane," said Buddha Ilford, cramming coarse dark brown tobacco into the bowl of his pipe.

"Can we have more light, sergeant?"

A faint nod from the Traffic super, and the overalled officer swung a high-powered inspection lamp into position above the block.

"Engine number 6–47X2–7, exactly as the registration book." Thane pointed to the lettering as the others pressed around him. "You've examined the chassis, sergeant?"

The man nodded. "Chassis and engine numbers match, sir."

Dan Laurence scratched his chin. "We'll just get a few wee photographs of that right now," he decided. "Willie—" The Bureau cameraman stepped forward with his equipment, took time over a series of shots, and pronounced himself satisfied.

For the benefit of his audience, Thane explained: "We know this is a faked number. Whoever put it there slipped up by choosing what he thought would probably be a number in the same engine series, but in fact was one allocated after the factory had modified the unit. The original number's been buffed off—"

"But now we're going to get it back again," Laurence finished for him. "On you go, sergeant."

The sergeant-mechanic pulled protective goggles over his eyes, picked up the waiting power-tool, its black cable snaking, and set to work. The whine of emery-stone on metal filled the air, a torturing, penetrating sound which finally died in a sobbing wail. The tool head was changed for a finer, polishing disc, and the noise began again but on a finer pitch. At last, the man was satisfied, and stood back.

"My turn to do some work for a change." Laurence took the small black bag handed him by his assistant, and opened it. Pulling on a pair of rubber gloves, he gave a brief, tongue-in-cheek lecture.

"This is just one of those times when Willie and I here realise the benefits of our superior education compared with that of some other characters we know who can only run around waving handcuffs and batons. Now here we have a thing called metallurgy, which you probably think is the name of a horse. The original engine number was stamped into this engine block, then somebody filed it off again, and it disappeared from view. But it's still there—the molecular structure of the metal was shunted about by that original punching." He carefully uncorked a bottle, used its contents to soak a pad of cottonwool, and warned, "Keep clear o' this stuff—it burns." Slowly, carefully, he began to wipe the newly buffed metal's highly polished surface. "So we just rub on some of this etching fluid now, nice and even, like sun tan lotion . . ." he grunted, peered closely at the metal, and was satisfied. "There's both your numbers, Thane—old and new. Bring that light a bit nearer, and see for yourself."

The etching chemical had trapped a continuing faint outline of the substitute number. But, strong and clear be-

low the phony 6–47X2–7 a new set of figures had appeared
—6–42X8–6.

At that moment, Mr. Putter would have been very unhappy to learn that his car had just ceased to belong to
him. It was the legal property of the insurance company
who exactly three months previously had had to pay out
eight hundred pounds, its insured value against theft. The
car's original shade of hyacinth blue remained unaltered.
But new number plates, white-wall tyres, and over-riders
were only a few of the detail changes which had altered its
appearance. By a quirk of fate, Mr. Putter had only himself to blame for his sudden return to the status of
pedestrian.

"Thanks, Dan." Thane finished his inspection, the moves
to come already falling into place in his mind.

"Call it natural genius, laddy," the bushy-haired Bureau
man said modestly. "Well, we'll give the chassis the same
treatment now—you'll have other things to do, eh?"

"Very interesting." Buddha Ilford stuck the pipe in his
mouth, struck a match, and sent billowing blue clouds of
smoke skywards. The pipe drawing to his satisfaction, he
turned to the others. "Well, let's have that talk, eh?"

Superintendent Beam had already had a room cleared
in the main building. The Traffic Department, well organised
in such affairs, had a scratch lunch of coffee and thick-cut
sandwiches waiting for their temporary guests. The Superintendent saw them settled, and left.

"Now then," Ilford knocked the ash from his pipe and
took a sandwich. "What's your plan, Colin?"

Thane took the plunge. "I'd like to buy a car, sir—with
a dud cheque, of course."

"Eh?" The sandwich halfway to his mouth, the C.I.D.
boss blinked. "Let's start at the beginning. How much do
we know about the car we've got—the one out there."

"Right, sir." Thane took a gulp of coffee, and began.

"We've two main streams, the car and the registration book. We know the car was stolen three months ago. A month later, Putter buys it from Bacarro Motors." He waited while Phil Moss passed the purchase receipt and registration book across the table to the once more impassive Ilford. "When Phil phoned in after seeing Putter I checked the company register. Bacarro Motors was formed less than a year ago with minimum registered capital and only two named directors, a George Liscomb and Benjamin MacGhee. So far, we've nothing on Liscomb. But MacGhee is an under foreman at Ascension Motors and also happens to be Erick Millan's top racing mechanic."

"Your first link," agreed Ilford, reaching for another sandwich. He passed the plate to Moss. "Inspector . . ."

"No thanks, sir." The Millside second in command was going easy where food was concerned.

"Suppose we take it for a moment that Liscomb and MacGhee are purely covering for young Millan." Thane flipped over the leaves of his notebook. "Now here's the vital part of it, sir. The registration book. We've got a genuine book and a genuine registration number—issued six months ago, three clear months before that car was stolen."

Ilford frowned. "This is the bit I can't follow," he admitted. "Putter's listed as second owner. You went to see the first owner, Moss . . ."

"And found he didn't exist," confirmed the C.I.D. man. "The address was real enough—an old bomb site off London Road."

"Then the car that was registered?" Ilford began to see the pattern develop. "Did it exist?"

"I don't think so." Thane turned to the notebook again. "There's a set drill for registering a new car, sir. The owner —or the garage acting for him—applies to the local Motor Taxation office. The application form lists the chassis and

engine number, and it has to be accompanied by an ac-
credited motor agent's sales delivery invoice. The Taxation
people keep a pretty sharp eye on the business, but if they
get an application and invoice from a firm they know, well,
they issue the registration book. They keep the application
and the delivery invoice on file. According to their records
the invoice for 641 WGG—our phantom car—came from
Ascension Motors and was signed by the sales director, Mr.
Erick Millan!"

Once again, Buddha Ilford went through the automatic
routine of filling and lighting his pipe. Teeth clenched on
its stem, he was deep in the contemplative thought to which
he owed his nickname. The two detectives could do little
but wait.

At last, the pipe was removed. "What you're saying is
that Erick Millan has been making false applications for
the registration of nonexistent vehicles, complete with details"—Ilford emphasised the point with a stab of the pipe-
stem—"complete with details that must be officially entered
in the registration book. Details of colour, make, and engine
and chassis numbers."

"There's little trouble in supplying the numbers, sir," declared Thane. "All he had to do was choose figures close to
those listed on some of the genuine cars being delivered to
Ascension."

"Probably," agreed Ilford dryly. "At the same time, I
suppose there probably is a car somewhere that does have
that number 6–47 whatever it is?"

"Probably. Though it's going to take time to trace."

"Hardly matter." Ilford waved the pipe again. "So Millan
gets a registration book, a passport to the perfectly open
sale of any car that matches that description!"

Thane nodded. "All he has to do is keep the book for a
few months, have one of his little gang steal a car that's
the same model, the same year, and the same colour as the

listed details, put on new plates and change it around a little—then sell it through Bacarro Motors."

At his side, Phil Moss was picturing just what that all entailed. A year had passed since Erick Millan had formed Bacarro Motors. For the moment, there was no telling how soon thereafter he'd begun acquiring registration books, allowing them to mature, keeping an eye open for the men needed to operate his plan. At first, probably, the new showroom would operate on perfectly legally acquired stock. Then, gradually, the change-over.

"It's just about a year since Millan was kicked out of that 'works' racing team," he mused. "That's what probably started it all."

Buddha Ilford gave a snort. "Money to keep going? Well, it could be the motive. All right, what's our next move— and that's taking it you're both remembering Bell's murder. Before, I held you back because we needed to break the car theft ring. Now, it could be the other way round."

He had pointed to their one remaining weakness, a weakness which, for the moment, Thane couldn't cure. "I'm in no hurry," he said softly. "That's why I want to buy that car, one from Bacarro Motors' current collection. At the same time, we'll wait and make sure that once Menran's finished altering their latest acquisition Carson delivers it to the showroom. But once that's done, sir, I say we act—go straight in bull-headed, grab the bunch, search their three bases—Menran's garage, the showroom, and the Ascension place." A grim hint of what lay in store for the car-theft accomplices lurked behind his next words. "Beat five men over the head with a murder charge, and one of them's going to talk. Even if the others hold out for a spell, MacGhee's the man most likely to crack. That's a very unhappy individual." He had put his cards on the table. Now it was up to Ilford. "Well, sir, do I buy that car?"

Once again, Chief Detective Superintendent Ilford took

his time about answering. The delay had nothing to do with indecision. Instead, he was remembering a day almost twenty years back, even before he got his division, when he'd landed an equally wild proposition in his boss's lap. It had amounted to trampling through the neatly laid garden of rules and procedure then, even before such items as detective training colleges and written thesis on the structure of evidence had been dreamed of. Against the modern background of legal and scientific precision, Thane's plea came close to heresy.

Twenty years back, the then C.D.S. hadn't wasted words in his answer. Buddha Ilford saw no reason for change.

"Do what you think right—I'll back it. And Lord help us all if you're wrong."

Thane gave a faint sigh of relief. "Thanks, sir."

"Don't thank me." The C.I.D. chief didn't bother to explain. "By the way, who's going to have the honour of buying this car with the rubber cheque? You or Moss?"

Thane grinned. "Neither. I've someone else in mind. A lady, sir—you could call her a friend of Inspector Moss."

CHAPTER SIX

Ida Murdock was delighted to help. She said so when Thane first contacted her by telephone at two o'clock in the afternoon. She repeated the fact at considerable length to an extremely wary Phil Moss who, despite all protests, found himself delegated to collect Miss Murdock by car from her suburban home and bring her into the city.

They rendezvoused with Thane at a café two short street lengths away from Bacarro Motors' showroom. The inevitable jukebox, fed coins by two pony-tailed young office girls, blared raucously in the immediate background as the Chief Inspector went yet again over the details.

"You're acting the part of a woman who has been left some money by an old aunt who died a little while back. Use your own name and address, but you know nothing about cars or the motor trade—though, of course, you've got a driving licence. And you've decided to buy a car. Right?"

Miss Murdock giggled and fingered one lapel of her lightweight yellow two-piece. The colour was startling, the effect heightened by her high-crowned black straw hat and a pearl choker necklace. A powerful waft of perfume accompanied her every movement. "I would have worn black if I'd known."

"She was a very distant aunt," amended Thane patiently. "You've got the chequebook, Saturday's evening paper with

Bacarro's advert, and your heart is set on buying the Triumph Herald they're offering. If they try to steer you on to a more expensive car, you're not interested."

"But if I've been left all that money, why can't I spend more of it?" Plump cheeks quivering with amusement, she looked appealingly across the table.

"Two reasons. First, the Triumph could be one which was stolen three weeks ago. The colour scheme is coffee and cream, which matches the original. Second, the price is the top limit the bank have authorised us."

"But you're going to stop the cheque anyway."

Thane shrugged. "Blame the bank, not me. They're pretty unhappy about the whole idea. And remember—once you've bought the car, you want to drive it straight away. If they stall you on insurance, you point out they advertise that they can offer immediate cover. Happy?"

"We-ll." Miss Murdock's eyes flickered mischievously. "I could think of a better story. Inspector Moss could come with me—we could be getting married, and the car would be a wedding present."

Phil Moss cringed from the idea, explaining rapidly: "The story about the aunt's better. Chief Inspector Thane or I might be spotted, Miss Murdock. . . ."

"Ida—please."

"Ida . . . anyway," he gulped, "it's too late now to make changes in the plan."

She sighed. "Oh well, it was just a thought. Shall I go now?"

Thane nodded. "And remember, there's nothing to worry about. Afterwards, we'll meet as arranged."

Waiting in the C.I.D. duty car, parked close by the café, the two detectives had first word of her progress a few minutes later. From his post within an apparent delivery van parked a few yards along from the showroom, Sergeant

MacLeod reported by radio: "Woman in a yellow dress just entered."

Cramped in the rear of the apparently deserted van, eyes fixed to the tiny observation peephole, it was another half hour before he sent his next message. "Woman now driving off in two-tone Triumph Herald."

From the duty car, Thane answered. "Thanks, sergeant. No other activity? Over."

In bored tones, MacLeod's voice came crackling back. "Nothing yet, sir. How long do we keep the van here? We could become conspicuous if we stay too long. We've been here two hours already. Over." Three days leg-work checking on wrecked cars, only to have the lot thrown in the bucket—and now observation duty. Detective Sergeant MacLeod felt far from happy.

"Remain on post until instructed." Thane spared a grain of sympathy. "We're fixing up a fixed point watch, Mac, but it takes a little time. Over and out." He pushed the car's microphone back into the dashboard pocket, and glanced at his watch. "She shouldn't be long now, Phil."

"Probably takes twice as long choosing a hat," Moss glowered through the window. "There's Tiny Watts. Wonder what he's up to these days?"

The assault and robbery merchant in question, out for a perfectly innocent stroll to the local bookie's, had seen the car. Now he caught Moss's glare, decided on a change of destination, and quickened his stride, heading in the opposite direction.

"Watts?" Behind the wheel, the C.I.D. duty driver stirred. "He came out about three weeks ago, didn't he? Oh—there's your car now, Chief Inspector." He pointed ahead. The little coffee-and-cream coupé nosed round a nearby corner, took a right turn into their street, and came slowly towards them, coasting the last few yards before halting at the pavement's edge. Ida Murdock levered her generous form from the driver's seat, crossed the pavement, and climbed into the rear of the police car, beside Moss.

"Oh . . ." she seemed breathless for a moment. "I wouldn't do that again, not even if you gave me the car to keep. I'm trembling all over."

"Any hitches?"

She brightened. "No . . . none at all. Of course, I was a wee bit worried when the salesman said they'd have to phone the bank to make sure the cheque was good—otherwise I'd have had to wait until it was cleared before they let the car go."

"We warned the branch that might happen," said Thane. "They knew what to say."

"Well, now . . ." the woman delved into her handbag. "Here's the receipt, and the registration book, the car keys . . . oh, and your chequebook back." She handed over the collection.

"Fine." Thane passed the keys to the C.I.D. driver at his side. "Take Miss Murdock's car to Helen Street yard—some of Superintendent Laurence's team will be waiting. They know what to do. I'll drive our own car back to Millside."

"Right, sir." The driver obviously welcomed a change of vehicle. He got out, had the Triumph's engine started, and was away in a healthy-sounding exhaust note within a few seconds of the order.

"Nice-looking car." Thane eased round in the front seat. "Well, Ida, what did you think of the place?"

"Huh." Miss Murdock gave an unladylike snort. "Their stock looks good enough and most of it is obviously low-mileage stuff. Yet I wouldn't deal with that firm at the other end of a barge-pole. They've got all the fittings, of course—fluorescent lighting, contemporary decoration, and salesmen with that newly laundered look about them. Cars have the inevitable three-month guarantee—but I know enough about the car business to get the feel of the sort of place it is. Make a sale, and then to hell with the customer, that's the motto with these boys. Even if their stock was straight-forward instead of stolen, it's still the sort of place that ends up giving the whole trade a bad name."

"The three-month guarantee's bound to give some protection," said Moss mildly.

Ida Murdock gazed at him tenderly. "You don't know much about the business, do you? There's guarantees, and guarantees. The kind they offer is a liability." She took a small enamelled silver cigarette case from her handbag, fitted a cigarette to an equally small black holder, and accepted a light. "Thanks. I don't smoke very often"—she gave that now familiar giggle—"but I think I deserve this one. Guarantees, now. When you get a used-car gurantee from a reputable firm it obviously means something, shows that they've gone over the car and are really backing it with their own good name. If something does go wrong, well, they supply the parts and you may have to pay for the mechanic's time involved or you may not.

"But a bunch like your friends back there use it as just another money-making racket. They slap a guarantee on the car without worrying about whether it is in good mechanical condition or not—ask my brother Sam, he's come across them before."

"Then what's the point of it?" queried Thane.

"Just this. You buy a car, something goes wrong with it, and of course, you bring it back to them to be repaired under that guarantee . . . which says you only pay for labour. That labour bill, when you get it, is big enough to cover mechanic's time and the spares you're supposed to be getting free—with a profit added on for good measure. Two out of three—no, nine out of ten of the car owners wouldn't have a leg to stand on if they challenged it.

They'd be talked into thinking they'd really been done a big favour."

Ruefully, Thane examined the receipt form in his hands. "You're not all like this, are you?"

"Heavens, no!" Ida Murdock was suitably indignant. "We've got fly men and chancers like every other kind of business—maybe even a few more than some. But there are plenty of honest firms, believe me. The trouble is, it's only the ones who land in bother who hit the headlines."

"I know what you mean," murmured Thane. "We've got troubles of our own in that direction. Nobody wants to read about policemen who won't take bribes—but let some fool cop get himself in a mess and the public's gasping to hear about it." He glanced at his wrist watch, and slid over behind the wheel. "Time Phil and I were getting back to Millside. I'll have another car take you on from there home."

"Oh." Miss Murdock was obviously disappointed. As the car started off she settled back in the seat cushions, feeling more than a little sorry that her adventure was over.

On arrival at the police station, Thane first fulfilled his promise and saw Ida Murdock despatched homeward. Then, a considerably relieved Moss by his side, he went up to the C.I.D. section.

They had a visitor waiting. Jock Mills broke off his gossip with one of the two d.c.'s in the room and came towards them with a grin of triumph. "I'm here to deliver the goods —all the gen you wanted on Erick Millan."

"Come on through, Jock," Thane guided the young crime reporter into his own office, Moss at their heels, then closed the door.

"Well, let's see it," he invited.

Mills scratched his mop of red hair. "I don't know if this is how you'll want it. Phil said you needed a picture of everything Millan's done in the last week." He took a folded bundle of close-typed copy paper from his pocket, and handed it to the Chief Inspector. "I did it up like a timetable—there are gaps, of course, but it's the best I could do."

Thane perched himself on an edge of the desk, and began reading. The *Bugle* crime reporter had done a pretty comprehensive job, the final result no mean tribute to his interviewing ability. Starting the previous Monday, the timetable had ragged portions where periods of hours were left either blank or with an attached query. But there was a solid mass of information remaining on the racing driver's movements, the evenings speckled with the names of a number of women with whom he'd been seen out and about.

His face expressionless, Thane reached the last sheet, finished it, and glanced up. "Sure of your facts, Jock?"

The reporter flushed. "If it's on the list, it happened, Chief Inspector."

"All right, Jock—I didn't mean it that way. It's a first-class piece of work. Leave it with us, eh?"

Ruffled feelings smoothed, Jock Mills grinned and gave a mock salute. "I'll be waiting on the story," he warned.

"You'll get it." Thane waited until the reporter had left. As the door closed, he tossed the copy paper on to his desk, then let his fingers drum on the wood.

"He did a good job all right," he said bleakly. "He's also given us what amounts to an unbreakable alibi for Erick Millan."

It was his own mistake, and he admitted it. Set to catch a car thief via a murder, he'd achieved the first, nibbled round the second, and allowed his own personal convictions to project a firm conclusion from the few inadequate facts that existed.

"According to this, Millan spent most of Thursday evening at a show in town. After the show, he took the girl he was with for a drive, they had a meal at a hotel just beyond Loch Lomond, and he got back into the city again at one A.M., a clear hour after Sammy Bell's body had been found."

"He and the girl . . ."

"Not a hope, Phil. A Chief Constable's daughter has the same human frailties as the rest of us—but Jock's thrown in the fact that Millan gave his autograph to half the hotel staff." He slammed fist and palm together in bitter frustration. "All right, if it wasn't Millan, who the hell did do it? Who was the man in the car who picked Bell up outside that café?"

"MacGhee?"

Thane gave a growl of derision. "Wouldn't have the guts—unless Bell was going to take a sledge hammer to one of his engines. But Bell was killed because he was up to his neck in this hot car trade. Unless our luck's completely out, the preliminaries were at the Ascension garage."

Suppressing a faint belch of stomach-inspired emotion, his companion posed a new difficulty. "What about tomorrow's setup?"

"No change. We get Laurence's report on the second car, wait till the Peaceview Terrace job's moved—and then we go in as planned."

Bitter-eyed, Thane contemplated the bare, cream-painted wall opposite. They'd go ahead all right—he had no alternative.

At that moment Erick Millan was in an equally bitter but considerably more vicious state of mind. All the morning, from the time Old Ludd had delivered his verbal tongue-lashing and had followed it up by ordering him out, Millan had sat next door to him, hearing the other man's footsteps, his muffled voice, the occasional opening and closing of his room door.

For the moment, at any rate, his uncle seemed to be

holding his hand. Messengers entered Millan's office as usual with a variety of queries and problems to be dealt with, the mid-day mail was delivered—it was obvious that none of their staff knew of the storm between the two men. With one half of his mind Millan dealt with the routine of his job as sales director for Ascension. But only one thing mattered, settling the sudden crisis.

He had lunch, returned, and met Old Ludd Millan as the older man emerged from his own room. Old Ludd, features rigidly emotionless, walked straight past him without a word.

Millan took off his sheepskin jacket, hung it on the stand by the door, and began an aimless pace of the ten-by-twelve room. There could be only one solution, and, unfortunately, there was only one man who could help him in it.

He went out, slamming the office door behind him, and clattered down the iron stairway.

On the workshop level, the nearest mechanic was struggling with the task of fitting new brake-shoes to an elderly Morris saloon.

"Where's MacGhee?"

"Up front somewhere, Mr. Erick . . ." he pushed a lock of hair back with an oil-smeared forearm. "Probably having a look at that gearbox job—they're having hell's own job fitting the replacement."

Millan threaded his way through the workshop, ignoring the familiar activity around. The mechanic had been right. Ben MacGhee was down in the main bay inspection pit, peering up from beneath the squat bulk of a four-ton truck while, above, two assistants sweated over the delicate task of lowering the new gearbox so that the bolt-holes on its flanged lip coincided with their twins on the clutch shell.

"Just a wee fraction more to the right, now—steady—

hold it," he implored them. "Now we're there—ach, she's slipped. . . ." He stood back in disgust.

"Ben, leave it and come up here." Millan stood at the lip of the pit. "I need a word with you."

MacGhee frowned uncertainly. "Right now, Mr. Millan? We're in a bit of bother. . . ."

"Leave it."

The foreman mechanic wiped the worst of the grease from his hands on a piece of waste, and came up. "Keep on with it till I get back," he told the two men in the lorry cab. "You're almost there, anyway." He fell into step with Millan, following the other man across the workshop to the corner where the racing cars lay. There, they were alone— no one was ever allowed near the cars without Millan's express permission.

"What happened this morning, Mr. Millan—with you and Old Ludd, I mean?" MacGhee was impatiently eager, his whole manner one of concern. "It's been hanging over me like that damned four-tonner, waiting to know. I hung back a bit there because of the other lads. Is it all right?"

"Anything but." Millan brought out his cigarettes, and they took one each, MacGhee scratching a match to life on the concrete floor.

"You mean he knows about—about the cars?"

"I don't know how much he knows," said Millan, letting the tobacco smoke drift from his nostrils. "He's got us taped as far as the racing budget's concerned, he grilled me about the Bacarro showroom . . . and my bet is that what he doesn't know he's having a ruddy good try at finding out."

Shakily, MacGhee raised the cigarette and drew hard on its tip. "What's he going to do? Would he—has he enough for the police?"

"Maybe." The race driver shrugged. "For a day or so at any rate I'm on suspended sentence. After that, it depends completely on how the old fool decides. I'm not relying on any long-shot chances. We're going to have to take care of him . . . and make sure that it's permanent." Every word was filled with open menace and intent.

"There might be some other thing we could do—make him see he had to keep quiet. Perhaps"—the mechanic had a sudden, desperate inspiration—"perhaps we could tell him the stink would wreck his own business. He'd listen to that."

"Old Ludd?" Millan's handsome features twisted in a crooked sneer. "That sanctimonious devil would go through hell on a bicycle if he made up his mind it was the right thing to do. I know the way he ticks. . . . I've had him peering over my shoulder ever since I was a kid, ready to rap my knuckles if I stepped out of line. He's got to be stopped before he makes trouble—and that could be any time after tomorrow."

MacGhee stared at him. "We—we couldn't get away with it."

"You know the alternative if he talks. You're not a young man any more, Ben. You'd be a lot older by the time you got back out of jail—and what about your family while you were inside? It could be rough."

"Maybe one of the others—Carson, or even Liscomb?" The other man swallowed hard, his face a pale parchment.

"No." Millan was ice-cold and deliberate. "It's going to be another accident, Ben. And it's going to happen here—the obvious place. A garage can be very dangerous to walk around in if you're at all careless . . . there's plenty of choice. That's why it has got to be you and me, Ben. Mainly you—because you could so easily arrange some of these things."

"It's the risk," muttered MacGhee. "What if . . ."

"Never mind the 'ifs,'" Millan cut him short. "The racing team will be working this evening. You're due to start on the engine development, aren't you?"

MacGhee nodded. The group of Ascension mechanics who

formed Millan's special squad gathered every Monday evening to work on the two cars. He'd planned to start them on the first stage of preparing the new engine blocks. All that seemed far away now . . . a distant dream which had a nightmare in the foreground.

"Good. I'll be with you for part of the night. Keep them at it until the usual time, then, when they leave, hang back on some pretext. I'll return again, and we can get down to details. Just start thinking about it, Ben—the dangerous things that can happen in a place like this. The fatally dangerous ones in particular." Contemptuous of the other man's fears, Millan strode off, climbed the stairway, and went back to his office.

Lifting the telephone, he told the garage switchboard, "I'm going out . . . tell any callers to try again in about an hour."

At exactly three fifty-six P.M.—15.56 hours, as noted in the log at Headquarters Control—the telephone on Chief Detective Inspector Thane's desk gave a long, emphatic peal.

"Thane."

"Headquarters Control here, sir—Sergeant Vincent. We've had the 'standby' signal from Peaceview Terrace, and the observation van is moving in. They'll be—one moment, sir." There was a pause of seconds, then the same voice, quiet, unhurried, resumed. "Fox Four, the unit outside Bacarro Motors, is also calling, sir."

Tie loosened, in his shirt sleeves, a ragged pile of scrawled and rejected pencil notes before him, the Millside chief abandoned torturous theory for practical action.

"Sergeant, can you patch through a relay?"

"It's ready when you are, sir."

Thane slammed down the phone, and scrambled from his chair. "Phil . . . they're surfacing!" His shout penetrated the thin partition between the two small office rooms. Phil Moss was at his heels as he hurried downstairs, through the uniform bar, and across to the radio section. The duty officer looked up as they entered.

"Patching through now, sir," he reported. "Normal direct relay procedure."

"I'll take it." Thane squeezed into the vacated chair, flipped the "send" switch, and moved the table microphone a fraction closer.

"Millside waiting—go ahead Control." He fingertipped the switch.

"Control to Millside. Fox Four and Fox Two standing by. Fox Two has Peaceview description and is mobile. All cars—all cars. Restrict to urgent service messages. It's yours, Millside." The Headquarters controller went off the air, still monitoring, but for the time being only a link in the radio chain.

"Millside to Fox Four, Sergeant MacLeod. Over." Thane waited.

"Four—MacLeod, sir." The signal was comparatively weak. Sergeant MacLeod's van was encountering considerable screening, parked as it was under the lee of a high tenement. "Party One arrived, driving his own car. He's gone inside the showroom. Over."

So "Party One"—the coding allocated against Millan because of too many newspaper offices having short-wave receivers with straying band-selectors—had turned up at last! For the first time Thane had Millan firmly located at the Bacarro showroom.

"Stand by, Four, come in Fox Two. Over."

"Fox Two." It was an unfamiliar voice, a Central Division d.c. "Following Austin car now bearing registration plates 249 KGG heading east along Dumbarton Road. Driver Party Three. Over."

A faint smile of satisfaction wisped across Thane's face.

Millan's arrival at the Bacarro showrooms was now no accident. Puggy Carson was moving the stolen Austin, and "Party One" obviously wanted to inspect their latest acquisition.

"East . . ." Moss consulted the big wall-map. "He should turn off at Byres Road, then over Queen Margaret Drive."

As if echoing him, the radio speaker boomed to life. "Fox Two to Millside. Now entering Byres Road. Over."

Thane raised a triumphant thumb. "Right in the net." He flicked the send switch again. "Fox Four—Mac, it's 249 KGG, coming your way. Fox Two, break off in sight of destination, and Four will complete. Over."

The two vans acknowledged, and went silent. A Southern Division patrol car nipped in with a quick request for an ambulance—the crew had a double gassing on their hands. Control acknowledged, and then the set settled to a quiet hum. The minutes crawled past.

"Fox Two to Millside. Message timed 16.25 hours. In sight of destination. Breaking off contact. Over."

"Fox Four. I've got him, sir." MacLeod waited. "He's gone into the rear of the building. Over."

"Roger. Millside to Fox Four, thank you. Fox Two, I'll leave it to you, Mac—and the fixed point observation team should be about ready to relieve you. Millside to Control, handing back now. Out."

He rose, and stretched luxuriously. "And that's that, Phil. We'll wait until the lab comes through with the report on Ida Murdock's Triumph—which is a foregone conclusion. Afterwards . . ." he gave a wry grimace, "a few prayers might be helpful."

At ten minutes past five Dan Laurence confirmed that the Triumph was on the "stolen" list. The car's second registration book was one issued under a delivery invoice signed by Erick Millan.

At ten P.M. the back-shift teams took over at the observation points.

At six A.M. they were relieved again.

In between these times a man died.

At exactly eight-fifteen A.M. the raids began, and with them, Thane's gamble.

Puggy Carson was first on the list. As the two squad cars drew to a halt in the quiet, tree-lined street outside the boardinghouse, a plain-clothes man crossed the road towards them.

"Still no sign of him leaving, sir," he reported, as Thane and the other officers emerged on to the pavement.

The little procession mounted the short flight of steps. Thane rang the doorbell, and eventually the door was opened by a maid, her dress and apron neat but her hair still tightly rolled in metal curlers.

"Police. Mr. Carson been down to breakfast yet?"

The girl gaped at them for a moment. "No, sir. I think he's still asleep."

"Where's his room?" Thane stepped into the hallway.

"First floor left—number seven. Will—will I tell him you're here?"

"No need."

They trooped upstairs to number seven. Gently, slowly, Thane eased the handle, then threw the door open, slamming it back on its hinges.

Still in his pyjamas, Puggy Carson was in the act of plugging his electric razor into the power socket above the room's washbasin. He jerked round, letting the razor fall to the carpet.

"Oh hell. . . ." he gauged his chances of making a bolt, decided he'd have to climb over a wall of cops in the process, and accepted the inevitable.

"Carson, we're police officers and . . ."

He waved the customary caution aside, and flopped down on the unmade bed. "I thought it was too good to last," he admitted. "But you might have waited until I had m'breakfast."

Thane was in no mood for pleasantries. "Two of you wait here, get him dressed, then bring him along. We'll leave one car. Give the room a going-over while you're at it."

Carson scratched the bristle on his cheeks. "Any idea what you're looking for, copper?"

"Evidence, Carson. Evidence to murder." The Chief Inspector growled the words.

"Gawd!" As a professional, Puggy Carson didn't particularly worry at the thought of another stretch in jail. It was nothing more than a business risk. But murder was different. . . . "Not me, copper! That's well out of my league," he protested.

Thane was already on his way from the room. The two detectives remaining stood expressionless. Puggy sighed, and reached for his shirt.

At Peaceview Terrace, Detective Inspector Phil Moss was having a slightly more difficult time. His two cars waited two blocks away from their goal until the Marine Division lookout reported Jacko Menran's arrival to Control. On the radioed go-ahead, the cars swept in, along Peaceview Terrace, bouncing straight up the narrow lane, coming to a halt blocking the big double doors of Menran Auto Electrics. While some of his squad fanned out round the building, Moss hammered on the wood.

"All right, Menran, we know you're in there. Police— open up."

He heard a scramble of feet within, the sound of smashing glass, and then shouts and a cry of pain. Moss sprinted round to the rear of the building. The glass window was shattered, and beside it a burly detective was half-carrying another of the squad clear. The injured man's eyes were stark with pain, and his right arm hung useless from the shoulder.

"Watch it, sir," warned his mate. "The bloke was half-way out the window when we saw him. He dropped back inside again—Joe tried to go after him, and got belted with a ruddy great iron bar."

Hugging the wall, Moss moved until he was standing inches to one side of the window frame. "Menran . . ." from within, he heard the faint clink of metal. "Menran, don't be a fool. There are six of us out here, and you're on your own. Just climb out quietly, and there won't be trouble. Menran . . ." cautiously, he pressed nearer to the shattered window, then a fraction further, trying to see within.

A blurred streak of grey, the iron bar flashed down, close enough for him to feel the wind of its passing. The sharp tip gouged a ragged splinter from the sill, raw wood showing white beside the dingy paintwork.

Seeing no sense in that kind of argument, Moss retired a few feet, sizing up the building.

Above and around, windows creaked open in the tenement block as families poked their heads out to get a better view of what was happening at ground level.

"Here—what's going on?" shouted a grey-haired pensioner, leaning over at a precarious angle from his top-storey vantage point.

"Nothing to worry about," replied the nearest detective. "Just keep indoors for a bit, Pop. This won't take long." Which he hoped was not being too optimistic.

The garage building was oblong, the shattered window at the rear having its counterpart on each of the two main sides. Moss stationed a man beside each window, baton drawn.

"If Menran as much as shows an inch outside, thump him," he ordered. "One hospital case is enough."

The injured C.I.D. man was sitting on the ground now, his back against the tenement wall. One of the Marine observation team was with him. The other had already telephoned for an ambulance. Moss returned to the front of the garage, spoke to the driver of the first police car, then briefed the remaining members of his squad.

The car's engine started. It reversed a few feet, then, accelerating, came forward, its bumper thudding against the closed garage doors in an elephantine nudge. The doors shivered, and cracks appeared in the wooden frame. Again the car reversed, and then lurched forward. This time, the doors shook and there was the sound of splintering.

"Now." Moss signalled. The police driver gave the car a slightly longer run, engine bellowing. Smashing against the double doors, the bumper sent them flying inward— and as the car stopped, Moss and his men poured through on either side.

Jacko Menran crouched in one faraway corner, the iron bar raised—then he dropped it, clawing frantically at his eyes as two of the C.I.D. men turned the cars' fire extinguishers on him, the foam jets stinging as they took him square in the face. There was a brief scuffle, then Menran was jerked upright, hands cuffed behind his back.

"Take care of him," said Moss to the two detectives gripping Menran's arm.

With a quick glance at his watch he headed for the second of the waiting cars, squeezed in beside the other occupants, and was still settling back when it started off. A quarter of a mile on, they passed an ambulance heading for Peaceview Terrace. Just about the same moment, Detective Sergeant MacLeod was leading in his own sortie, a quiet, incident-free affair at Bacarro Motors. He collected Liscomb, left a guard on the three bewildered salesmen and was about to leave when he had a sudden thought. Going back into Liscomb's office, he wrote quickly on a sheet of paper, spread gum along one edge, and took his handiwork out to the main door. With considerable care the sergeant centred the notice on the glass, then stood back with a grin to admire the result.

The notice bore one word. "Closed."

CHAPTER SEVEN

Ascension Motors opened for business at eight-thirty, but it was five past nine before Erick Millan drove his blue-and-red two-seater into the garage. In a newsagent's shop opposite, a young woman with a shopping basket stopped her apparent inspection of the array of magazines, showed a police warrant card, then used the proprietor's telephone.

Three minutes later, a combined force of four C.I.D. cars plus the Scientific Bureau's mobile unit and a patrol van loaded with uniformed constables were deployed around the one-time cinema. In the garage forecourt, a protesting pump attendant found himself being gently but firmly ushered into the main building while two uniformed men took his place, ready to turn away any would-be customers.

Dan Laurence trailing a few steps to the rear, Thane and Moss walked through the main repair shop, heading for the stairway leading to the office level above. As they passed, mechanics stopped their work, gathering in small groups to murmur together as they saw a steadily growing number of police appearing throughout the building.

Old Ludd Millan met the trio as they reached the top of the stairway. Jaw outthrust, he barked, "What the blazes is going on here? There'd better be a good reason for this invasion, Thane." He stood there, hands clenched on the balcony rail, a tired but angry grey-haired giant, scowling as he took in the scene below.

"We've a search warrant—that's reason enough." Thane took the folded paper from his inside pocket. "And I'm looking for your nephew—and MacGhee. Where are they, Mr. Millan?"

Old Ludd stayed silent, his grip tightening on the balcony rail until the knuckles showed white.

"Your nephew, Mr. Millan . . ." Thane persisted.

"I'm here—what do you want, anyway?" Erick Millan had emerged from his office. He stood in the open doorway, initial annoyance fading to indecision under Thane's quiet, unruffled inspection.

The Chief Inspector's words came hard and cold as ice-chips. "For the moment, just to know where you are, and to make sure that you stay there. We've work to do here—but after that, I'm going to line you up with the rest of your gang, MacGhee, Carson, and Menran, and Liscomb. I'm charging you with the theft and reset of motor cars and the uttering of false papers for the purpose of obtaining motor registration documents. I'm only cautioning you, Millan—the charge comes later. For one of you, it may be a much graver list."

Millan's mouth twitched. "You're crazy."

Phil Moss slid a practised finger-and-thumb-twist grip on the racing driver's right sleeve. "We don't think so, Millan. We've already collected the others—there's only you and MacGhee to put in the bag. The other three are on their way here now, all ready for a long talk."

"Never heard of them." Millan glared down at his sleeve and jerked his arm. The grip remained.

"It's not worth trying, Millan," said Thane softly. "We've already identified two of the cars you processed. At this moment there's a squad checking every car in the Bacarro showroom."

Flushed and vicious, Millan turned on his uncle. "I suppose all this—this madness—is due to you, you—"

Old Ludd flinched, then slowly shook his head. "No, you're wrong, Erick. I haven't spoken yet—to police or anyone else." Still partially numbed by the shock of the raid, he frowned down at the search warrant lying unopened in his hand. "I'll phone our lawyer and get him over. Unless" —a flash of his usual spirit put bite into the words—"unless you've any objection, Chief Inspector?"

"He hasn't been charged yet," shrugged Thane.

"In that case," countered the older man, "there's no need to grip him like that, is there?"

At Thane's slow nod, Phil Moss released his hold. The Chief Inspector gestured to one of the C.I.D. men who had joined them on the balcony. "Take him back into his office, and keep him there." As the man obeyed, Thane turned his attention to the workshop floor below. "We'll get MacGhee now."

Dan Laurence cleared his throat. "Eh—I think I'll come down with you, Colin. Time my boys got to work—we know what we're after."

A second plain-clothes man joined Millan and his escort as the three senior officers went back down the stairway. At the balcony rail, Old Ludd spread open the search warrant and began to read. Halfway through, he swayed, steadied himself, then turned and went back into his office.

Below, Dan Laurence headed off in search of his "boys," who had already begun wriggling under some of the cars lying in the "Staff Only" parking bay. Thane tried the nearest group of mechanics, standing idle, still puzzled at the cause of the eruption into their working routine.

"Where's MacGhee?" he demanded. "Seen him about?"

"Ben?" The oldest of the group took a last drag at his cigarette while he considered. "No—not so far this morning. But he's around. His car's over there—that old grey Vauxhall."

"Sam was lookin' for him a wee while back," volunteered

another of the men. He turned: "Hey, Sam, fella wants you."

The mechanic called Sam lounged across from a nearby bench.

"We're looking for MacGhee," Thane began again.

"You're not alone, mate," said Sam with a shrug. "Charlie an' me can't get started till he shows up. We've been sittin' on our backsides since half eight waitin' on him."

"Why? What's the matter?"

"Nothin' much. We're havin' a bit of a wrestle, like on a job. Got fouled up in it yesterday, so Ben says wait till he comes in this mornin' and he'll fix it." The mechanic waved one hand expansively. "He's likely slept in—we'd a late night of it, an' him more so."

"In here?"

"Aye, on the cars. You know, the racin' stuff," explained the mechanic patiently. "I'm one o' the team. Saw you at the track on Sunday, too."

Without knowing why, Thane began to feel suddenly uneasy. "So last night some of you left before MacGhee?"

"We all did, about ten. Just Ben stayed on. Said he'd have another wee look at somethin'—hell, I'm keen enough, but he's got these ruddy cars worse than religion."

"Thanks." Frowning now, Thane turned. Phil Moss had drifted over to another group of garage staff, but now he came back, shaking his head.

"It's a bit queer," he complained. "Seems MacGhee's normally in dead on time. Yet none of the rest of our birds could have tipped him off—they hadn't a chance."

Together, they walked across the width of the garage to the staff parking area and MacGhee's grey Vauxhall. Thane opened the bonnet and felt the radiator—it was stone cold. Inside, the key was still in the ignition switch.

"More trouble, Colin?" Dan Laurence, his suit covered by a linen dustcoat which already showed signs of black oil smears, emerged from under the next car. He had a powerful torch in one hand and a small scraper in the other.

"Could be." Thane traced a slow pattern on the dust-covered wing. "We can't find MacGhee—yet this is his car."

Laurence raised an eyebrow. "Maybe he left it here last night—he could be still at home. What about the outside watch—didn't they see him come in?"

Phil Moss answered. "Their only target was Millan. We had separate watches on Puggy Carson and Menran because of their link with the last of these stolen cars, and a fourth team keeping a general eye on the Bacarro showroom. But there was no special observation on either Liscomb or MacGhee. We collected Liscomb smoothly enough —and MacGhee would normally have been here by now."

They'd been up against the same old problem. Observation duty gobbles up police strength, and like most of Britain's recruit-hungry forces Glasgow was considerably under-manned. The detective force had to be spread thin over the area at the best of times, and if there was a possible way to economise in manpower it had to be taken.

"Well, might as well take a look at his car, then," said the Scientific Bureau chief. "You were right about that little sports job of Millan's—it's clean."

The other men of Laurence's team were similarly engaged around them, going through the process of examining the underside of each and every car. Before, at the police yard and at the Bacarro showrooms they'd been intent enough on their task. But now, with the emphasis turned from proving theft to seeking the car which killed Sammy Bell, they worked with a new, grim efficiency.

With a grunt, Laurence got down on the concrete again and wriggled his burly form beneath the Vauxhall, until only his feet projected into the open.

"Phil—" Thane was about to tell his companion to take a trip out to MacGhee's home. The order wasn't completed.

At that instant, there was a sudden shout, frantic in its urgency.

"Hey—over here, quick." A white-faced mechanic gestured furiously in their direction.

The two detectives sprinted over, forcing their way through the cluster of Ascension garage staff fast gathering round the four-ton truck straddled over the main inspection pit.

They'd found Ben MacGhee. Sam and Charlie, the two men who'd been waiting the foreman's arrival, gazed up from the darkened gloom of the pit floor.

"Down here, mate," said Sam tensely. He swung the inspection lamp in his hand, sending the beam into the black shadows beneath the truck.

Ben MacGhee lay face down on the grimy floor . . . the heavy weight of a replacement gearbox across his broken back.

Thane dropped down into the four-foot-deep pit then, crouched down, felt MacGhee's pulse. The wrist was cold and lifeless. It was up to the forensic experts to try to establish a time of death, but it had obviously been several hours previous.

"We decided we'd better get started, like," said Sam awkwardly. "Charlie an' me came over an', well, the gearbox jist wasnae there. We thought it'd slipped—then we foun' the inspection lamp lyin' lit inside the truck cab. Ben must have tried to have a go at it himsel' last night." He pursed his lips. Scots mechanics aren't given to emotional displays. His next words formed a reasonably sympathetic requiem. "A dam' silly way to die."

Thane saw the empty loop of the tackle chain, hanging motionless above. "Phil. . . ."

Moss's face appeared in the yawning gap in the vehicle's floor. "Up here."

"He's dead," said Thane shortly. "Get Doc Williams on

the phone, and ask him to come right down. Then see if
that policewoman's still outside. If she is, take her along
with you."

"His wife?" Somebody had to do it. Somebody always
has, and when you were a cop it was part of the job. Moss
gave a slow, reluctant nod. "I'll put a man on guard up
here," he volunteered. "Want Dan Laurence over?"

Thane nodded. The thin face of the Detective Inspector
disappeared from the gap above, and there was a creak of
springs as he left the cab.

"Mister—" it was the second of the two mechanics beside him who spoke. "What did you want to see Ben about,
anyway?"

Looking up from the body, Thane saw the other man's
face, earnest yet querulous. "It doesn't matter much—now,"
he said quietly. "I'll need a word with you two later, but
for the moment just wait out there somewhere, will you?"

The two mechanics weren't loth to leave. On his own,
Thane swept the inspection lamp around the floor of the
pit, then, raising himself in an awkward knees-bent stance,
examined the gap between engine and prop shaft and then,
peering through the gap in the floor of the lorry cab,
checked the block and chain arrangement above. The chain
had been round the gearbox as a safety sling, its faraway
end anchored to a stout metal bracket inside the cab. An
additional support, obviously placed under the gearbox
when the men stopped work the previous evening but later
removed, was a four-by-two wooden batten, now lying to
one side on the cab floor.

The noise of someone scrambling down into the pit, accompanied by a muffled curse, brought Thane back to his
previous crouch. Dan Laurence gave another soft oath as
his head bumped against the lorry sump, then squatted
beside him.

"MacGhee?" The Bureau man was visibly perplexed.

"Hell's fire, Colin, it's impossible. It was his car that killed Bell!" He scratched his bush of white hair with considerable vigour. "There's clear traces under it, blood staining and the rest. We'll need to cross-match the groups, but that's hair-splitting stuff. Anyway, it's got the same type of tyre pattern—and now this! What the devil do you do now?"

Granite-faced, Thane digested the news in silence. Without asking, he knew that Laurence's squad would now be turning their whole attention to the Vauxhall. He looked again at the chain above his head, then at the gearbox which had snapped the life from the man lying under it.

"We can't move him until Doc gets here," he said, passing over the inspection lamp. "But there's a few things wrong about this, Dan."

"The way he's lying?" Laurence shrugged. "He could have been turning away when it fell, I suppose—" then he stopped, eyes narrowing as he peered more closely at the gearbox casing, holding the inspection lamp close to the metal. Thane moved back to give him room as the Bureau man turned his examination to the noosed chain above.

"Another one, eh?" He gave his verdict in a flat, matter-of-fact way. "You're right, Colin. That hunk o' metal may have been what killed him—but it didn't slip."

The whole gearbox casing was painted a dark olive-green, intended by the factory to distinguish it as a re-conditioned rather than a brand-new unit. There were one or two scratch marks in a rough band round the casing where the chain must originally have gripped . . . but none of the long, more general scraping which would obviously have occurred if the heavy weight had slipped and grated its way free from the chain loop. There were other signs too, something over-neat about the way in which MacGhee's body was lying.

Dan Laurence clinched it. "Ever seen a mechanic midway through a repair job who had perfectly clean hands?"

he asked sardonically, holding the lamp close to illustrate his point. "I don't know what MacGhee was doing, Colin, but he wasn't working when this happened."

Somebody had tried hard to be clever . . . the inspection lamp lying burning, the slipped chain, even, Thane noted, one or two holding bolts left scattered around. In other circumstances, the bluff might have succeeded—just another unfortunate accident, to a man putting in an over-zealous spot of unofficial overtime. But the tide of luck had run out for that somebody—run out because he couldn't have guessed at the raid planned for that morning, or the entire atmosphere of suspicion clouding everyone and anything associated with the Ascension garage.

"Well . . . ?" Dan Laurence waited.

Almost reluctantly, Thane returned to the moment at hand. "We know MacGhee was working late last night. He stayed on after the others had left, saying he wanted to take another look at some item. From the signs, he was deliberately hanging back, and probably got cleaned up while waiting—probably waiting to meet Erick Millan."

"Can you prove it?"

The chief nodded. "The observation team can. If Millan came back here last night they'll have a note of it. They wouldn't report direct unless there was obvious reason, but they'll have logged it. That's one factor he couldn't have counted on."

There were footsteps above, and the murmur of voices. A plain-clothes man peered down. "Chief Inspector—the doctor's here."

"Ask him to come down." Thane helped Doc Williams scramble into the inspection pit. "You didn't waste much time."

The police surgeon was already beside the body, opening his leather instrument bag. "You, a body and this place

. . . that adds up to reasonable priority," he said. "What's the setup? Can I move this thing on top of him?"

"Not until Dan's boys have got their end of it tied up," Thane told him. "Keep it to a preliminary examination, Doc. But I want to know how this man died—in detail."

The medical man was immune to surprise. "Complications, nothing but complications," he grimaced. "Do you know I could be earning twice as much being a village G.P. somewhere and treating kids for measles?" He reached for the long blunt-nosed thermometer. "Well, I'll get on with it."

They left him to it, going from the pit back up to the workshop floor.

"I've plenty to do too, now," said Laurence, lighting a cigarette. He gave a snorting growl. "Doc's right, you know —complications, nothing but complications. I'll be around if you need me." He strode off to begin the task of redeploying his team.

Thane turned to the plain-clothes man, standing watchfully at the side of the truck. "Any of the observation team about?"

"Yes sir, D.C. Mahone—he's over by the main entrance."

He thanked the man, and headed in the direction indicated. Mahone had installed himself in the little reception booth and, inevitably, had an electric kettle on the boil with a commandeered teapot waiting alongside.

Yes, he agreed, he'd been on observation duty—one of the relief team who had taken over at six A.M. One eye on the kettle, now steaming merrily, he produced the notebook log.

"From ten last night onwards," said Thane. "That's the time segment we need."

"Right, sir." Mahone flicked the pages, then paused, pointing with one stubby forefinger. "Here we are—the last two entries before the change-over, sir."

Erick Millan was recorded as having arrived at the
Ascension garage at 22.45 hours. He'd left again just over
an hour later, at 23.52. From the time the racing team
mechanics had gone home, leaving MacGhee alone in the
building, Millan had been the only visitor.

"Thanks." There was a grim satisfaction to be gained from
the situation. "Mahone, when the other three arrive—Carson
and company—hold them here till I'm ready."

"Right sir—just a moment—" as the telephone gave a
sudden peal, the detective constable lifted the receiver. He
listened, then held out the instrument. "For you, sir."

Thane took the call. Phil Moss was at the other end,
and there was eager excitement in his low-voiced tone.

"Colin? I'm at MacGhee's home."

"How's his wife taken it?"

"Pretty badly," the reply came crackling. "The policewoman's with her, and a neighbour's fetching a relative
over. That's not why I'm calling—Dan Laurence told me
about MacGhee's car before I left."

"We've got further," Thane informed him. "MacGhee
didn't have an accident, Phil . . . it was well-rigged murder."

Moss gave a low whistle. "Can't say I'm surprised. Look,
I asked his wife about his not coming home last night. She
said it hadn't worried her particularly—seems once he got
working on those racing cars he was liable to stay to all
hours. Sometimes he'd just bunk down in the garage. But
this is the important bit. I asked her about last Thursday
night. She says MacGhee came home about eight, and
stayed in all evening—they had friends visiting who didn't
leave till after midnight. That lets him out for the Sammy
Bell killing, but there's more. Mrs. MacGhee says he wasn't
driving his own car—he brought Millan's home for the evening."

"Erick?" Thane snapped the word. "There's the alibi . . ."

"No . . . his uncle! Old Ludd complained that his car had been giving trouble, and told MacGhee to test-drive it around for a spell and try to spot the fault."

"And MacGhee's car?"

"She doesn't know. It was left at the Ascension place—she thinks. But MacGhee didn't seem to find anything seriously wrong with Old Ludd's machine." Moss paused. "Anything more I can do at this end?"

"Nothing at the moment," replied Thane. "Head back here, Phil—oh, and tell your policewoman to stall off Mrs. MacGhee if she suggests coming down to the garage. Right now, I'm going to have a talk with the Millans—a long talk."

He put down the receiver, nodded to the waiting detective, and went out, heading purposefully towards the stairway and the office level above. The garage staff had obviously given up the idea of any further work for the time being. A blue haze of cigarette smoke hung like a cloud above the wash bay, where most of them seemed to have gathered, their conversation punctuated by occasional mass growls of agreement with some particular suggestion put forward. Thane passed them by, climbed the stairway, went straight to Ludd Millan's room, and opened the door without bothering to knock.

Old Ludd's attractive, dark-haired secretary was alone in the room, busy sorting out a bundle of letters.

"Where's Millan?"

"Mr. Ludd?" She hesitated, her manner uneasy. "He—he went out a few minutes ago, sir. He said he had to see Mr. Erick—" the girl broke off, open-mouthed, as Thane stormed from the room.

In the next-door office, Ludd Millan was waiting, quiet, relaxed, standing by the opened window, an army issue .38 Webley revolver held loosely in one hand. Beside the big desk the detective who'd been left on guard lay sprawled unconscious on the floor—and Erick Millan had gone.

"Take it—" Old Ludd held out the gun, open-palmed. Thane ignored him, going down on his knees beside the injured officer. The man's pulse was strong, and the swelling on the back of his head told its own story.

"I didn't hit him very hard," the tall grey-haired garage owner was almost apologetic. "I'm sorry, Chief Inspector, but it had to be."

Thane rose, almost snatched the Webley from its holder, and hurried over to the window. Outside, a broad ledge ran a short distance along the side of the building, then joined on to a wide, flat roof. Beyond was the rear of the garage and beyond that again the start of a maze of back yards and buildings.

"He's got a five-minute start," said Old Ludd. "He'll be clear by now, Chief Inspector." Slowly, he moved away from the window and slumped into a chair. "He got clean away all right—I watched him go."

A dull, bitter knot inside him, Thane pulled the window shut and went into action.

Ludd Millan was right. For the moment, at any rate, his nephew had vanished. By the time Phil Moss reached the Ascension garage the first search of the immediate area was an acknowledged failure and the wider, city-enveloping net was already in process of being cast—bus and rail stations, airports, the whole of Clydeside's sprawling dockland came within its scope. Headquarters control had teleprinter messages chattering out to the city's seven divisional offices and their outlying sub-stations. Patrol cars had already been warned by radio, and the same message was now being relayed on to the neighbouring county forces: "Find Erick Millan."

Throughout the turmoil of activity Old Ludd remained

impassive and withdrawn. He showed only temporary interest as Doc Williams helped bring the stunned escort back
to consciousness. The detective was relatively unhurt, apart
from the bump on his head and an acute sense of embarrassed foreboding which made him look almost relieved
to be packed off to hospital for a further check-over. From
that policeman's point of view, the longer he could be kept
out of Colin Thane's path the better he'd like it.

At last, Thane re-entered the room, Phil Moss at his side.
He nodded to the uniformed man who had taken over as
replacement guard and the man left them.

"Well, Mr. Millan?" Thane's tone was bitter.

The man gave a wry smile. "It had to be, Chief Inspector.
Oh, maybe you'll catch him, and he deserves all that's
coming to him—but the boy's my nephew, Thane, the only
approach to family I've got. Once I read that search warrant
there was really no choice—"

Phil Moss glanced down at his notebook. "According to
our man, you came into the room and said you'd the Chief
Inspector's permission to talk to your nephew. When he
challenged that, you suggested he phone down to the reception office—that you'd just left the Chief Inspector there.
He remembers lifting the phone . . ."

"And then I tapped him on the head with that gun,"
completed Millan. "Don't worry about cautioning me, either
of you. I've nothing to hold back now."

"You may have yet," said Thane standing over the older
man's chair. "You read that search warrant—your nephew
was involved in much more than a hot car racket, Millan."

Surprisingly, the garage owner gave that same wry smile
again. "You played it very cleverly, Chief Inspector. How
long have you known Bell's death wasn't an accident?"

"Ever since a police driver called MacDonald took his
first look at the body. And now we've found blood traces

under Ben MacGhee's car, a car he wasn't driving that night."

Millan's lips tightened. "You can keep Ben MacGhee out of it, Chief Inspector. You see, I killed Sammy Bell . . . you've probably guessed that by now."

"Since we found MacGhee was driving your car, yes."

"Ben had nothing to do with it," emphasised Old Ludd.

"MacGhee's dead," said Thane harshly. "While you were letting Erick out of that window we found MacGhee's body in an inspection pit."

"Dead?" Millan whispered the word, his eyes wide with a fresh spark of horror. "You mean—"

"I mean he was murdered in this garage late last night at a time when the entire building was under observation. Only one man—one man"—Thane hammered the words home—"came and went during that time. The same man you helped to escape."

Old Ludd gave a faint moan. "Why? He—Erick needed Ben. These cars . . . it was MacGhee's skill as much as Erick's driving that made them successful."

"We don't know the answer to that." Thane walked three steps away from the chair, then turned. "But you know some answers, don't you, Mr. Millan?"

One hand rubbing nervously over his pale, shock-slackened face, Ludd Milan muttered: "Could I have a drink? There's water—in the carafe on that shelf."

Moss poured a glassful, and the two detectives stood silent while the other man drank.

"Thank you." Ludd Millan put down the glass. "I'm sorry about that. But—well, if Erick did kill MacGhee, Chief Inspector, that blame probably should be mine. Did they know that you were—"

Thane shook his head. "Supposing you tell us your side of it."

Ludd Millan agreed. "Yes, I want to make a statement

—a full statement, Chief Inspector. You see, I killed Sammy Bell . . . you've probably guessed that?"

"I was coming round to that," said Thane slowly. "Mr. Millan, before you go further I must formally caution you . . ."

Old Ludd nodded. "I know—I don't have to say anything, but if I do it can be taken down in writing. Well, if your inspector is ready with that notebook?"

Phil Moss settled in a chair beside the desk, pencil ready.

"It began last Wednesday, when Bell telephoned me at home," said the garage owner. "He said he wanted to see me privately, somewhere where we would be completely alone. Well, I asked him what it was all about—it was the first time we'd spoken apart from the odd occasion when I stopped by at the filling station. He more or less laughed, and said that I could 'ruddy well come along and find out, or it would be the worse for Erick.'" Millan gave a sigh. "You know I took Bell in, Chief Inspector, ignored his record and even let him live in that storeroom. Confronted like this, I wanted to know more, and I told him so. All he'd add was that I'd better meet him that same evening."

"You agreed?"

Millan nodded. "I saw him about an hour later. I drove round to a spot near the filling station and picked him up. He told me that Erick was running a stolen car business, and was actually organising the thefts, then selling the cars through a separate showroom he'd opened—Bacarro Motors. I told him he was mad, and then he became nasty. He said—well, I won't try to duplicate the language, but he gave me a car registration number and told me to check with Motor Taxation who had originally notified the sale in the application for a registration book—and then to check our own records and see if the transaction was listed. He said he wanted five thousand pounds as payment for keeping his mouth shut."

Over in the corner, Phil Moss's pencil flew as his short-hand battled to keep pace with the flow of words. As he finished the last sentence he looked up. "Blackmail?"

"Pure and simple," agreed the garage owner. "Bell said he had quarrelled with Erick—that he wasn't getting enough of a share from him. He had decided to get out, but he wasn't going empty-handed."

Thane took out a cigarette, lit it, then, a little of the harshness gone from his manner, gave one to Millan.

The garage man's hand trembled a little as he accepted a light in turn. Then he drew in deeply, let the smoke trickle free, and went on. "Bell phoned me the next afternoon—the Thursday—and by that time I'd checked the records and found that he was right. Erick had registered that car, but we hadn't sold it. By that time, too, I'd begun to realise that this might be where all the money was coming from for the racing team—something I'd never quite understood before." He allowed the cigarette to burn unheeded. "Try to understand, both of you. Erick's father and I were—well, more than brothers. We were friends, devoted friends. When first he died and then Erick's mother, that boy—"

"I can follow," said Thane quietly. "So you decided to kill Bell."

"What else?" Ludd Millan shrugged. "I'm just old enough to have been in at the tail end of the first war, and the start of the second. We killed to order then. This was a more personal thing, for I wasn't fooling myself, Chief Inspector. As long as Bell was alive he would keep on trying to bleed me of money and at the same time remain a constant threat to Erick. I'd some wild idea that if I could get rid of Bell then I could start after that on straightening Erick out, no matter how deeply he was involved.

"I told Bell I'd meet him that night, and he suggested the café in South Salisbury Street. When he'd hung up, I saw Ben MacGhee, and complained about my car. Ben agreed to take it home, and I joked that I'd just borrow his for the night."

"So you were in MacGhee's car when you kept the appointment with Bell?"

Old Ludd nodded. "I told him we'd have to go back to the garage to settle things up—I knew the place would be deserted at that hour. He wasn't very keen, but finally agreed. We drove here, I shut the doors behind us." His lips pursed. "I let him get a little way ahead, and then I hit him with the butt end of that gun—that's another charge, I suppose. It isn't licenced." The wry smile came and went. "I hit him hard, Chief Inspector, not a tap like I gave your man. Afterwards, I put him in the car boot and drove out to the filling station. It was closed, of course, but I had Bell's key. Well, I searched his room, in case he'd left anything behind which might incriminate Erick—but they're careful, these people. I took some papers—in fact, I still have them—but there was nothing concerning the stolen cars. So I locked up the place again, drove to South Salisbury Road, and the rest you know."

"And today?"

First Millan flicked the long white ash from the cigarette's tip, inhaled, and ground out the remaining stub. "When you came for Erick I thought that his time had simply run out. Then I saw the search warrant, and realised that in all probability you'd got on to him because of the very thing I did. The search warrant was for a murder weapon —and I had murdered Bell." He shrugged his massive shoulders. "I came in, hit your man on the head, then told Erick to get out. He wanted the gun, but I wouldn't give him it.

"There's—you're sure he killed Ben?"

"Beyond all reasonable doubt." Thane studied the shattered, broken man before him. "The police surgeon's preliminary examination shows that MacGhee was almost certainly killed by a blow on the back of the neck, delivered by some blunt instrument, probably soft-covered. Superintendent Laurence's men found a copper-headed mallet with a leatherbound striking surface—the type of tool used for freeing knock-off wheel hubs and similar jobs. It was hidden in the cockpit of one of the racing cars.

"There was no blood on it, of course—MacGhee's skin wasn't broken by the blow. But there were hairs clinging to the mallet head. There were fingerprints on the mallet handle. The hair looks as though it will cross-match with MacGhee's, and the prints match with samples we believe to be your nephew's. As we see it, they had a quarrel, MacGhee was killed in the heat of the moment, and then Erick tried to fake the death to look like an accident."

He put a hand on the other man's arm and raised him to his feet. "Time to go, Millan. But tell me, would you have let him go out of that window if you'd known that he was just like you—that he'd killed?"

Head bowed, the garage owner didn't answer.

CHAPTER EIGHT

"We're trying that, sir—yes, full road blocks requested. I'll keep in touch. . . ."

Somewhat red-faced, Colin Thane put down the telephone receiver and leaned back in the office chair normally used by Erick Millan. "That," he said ruefully, "was Buddha. And he isn't very pleased. I gather the Chief Constable has been saying rude things to him—and he certainly passed the bulk of it down the line."

Phil Moss gave a grunt. "They should be damn glad we've got this far." He jerked open yet another desk drawer and began dumping its contents by his side.

"Ach, he'll cool down," declared Thane. "But right now I'm not the most popular divisional chief on his strength. Oh, he's happy enough to get the Bell murder tidied up, and to know the car racket can be crossed off the list. But," he imitated Chief Superintendent Ilford's grumphing tone, "'Why the devil did you allow young Millan to walk out from under your nose, Thane? Getting him back is your baby—and you'd better have it nice and tidy before the papers cash in on the story.'"

"How long do you reckon that gives us?" Moss stirred through the batch of assorted items, ranging from a pack of grease-stained playing cards to a motor trade year-book, made a quick mental catalogue and dismissed the stuff as useless.

Thane shrugged. "Not long enough. Give it another couple of hours, and most of the newspaper offices will know something's on the boil. Buddha's already had one reporter on his doorstep and chased him off. Erick Millan's celebrity class, Phil—any news editor who has the tip we're looking for him is going to put every man he's got on getting the story."

"So?" Moss tried another drawer.

"My bet is that by the afternoon editions they're beginning to run anything they can. You know the sort of thing— 'Police are anxious to contact Mr. Millan, who may be able to help them in their inquiries.' They'll chance sticking their necks out. Old Ludd and the other three will have to appear in court for remand tomorrow, and from then on the cat's out of the bag."

"This one's locked." Moss gave a final despairing tug at the top right-hand drawer. "Want me to force it?"

"Be my guest." Thane passed him the long, heavy screwdriver borrowed from one of the Ascension tool boxes, then looked round as the office door opened and Sergeant MacLeod came in. "Well, Mac"—he snapped his fingers in sudden recollection—"hey, we've still got Carson and company outside."

"That's what I came up about, sir," said the sergeant. "Do you still want to see them? I mean, things have changed a bit, haven't they?"

"Things have," confirmed Thane. "But we may as well sort out their side of the picture. Where are they?"

"Waiting in the patrol van, sir. I've had it brought into the garage . . . oh, and the car which took Ludd Millan back to Millside has completed delivery. It's on its way back now."

"Better bring all three of them up here—" Thane halted as, with a final splintering crackle of wood and an accompanying growl of satisfaction, Moss succeeded in jemmying open the desk drawer. "Careful with them, though, sergeant. If we lose any more prisoners this whole division'll go straight on to the 'retired' list."

"Yes, sir." MacLeod went out, smothering a grin.

A gradual pile of items was built up on the desk as Moss emptied the newly forced drawer. Cheque stubs, a bank book, two rolls of cine film, a gold-plated cigarette lighter . . . he gave a sudden whistle of interest as, right at the back of the drawer, he found a small metal box, black-enamelled and locked.

"Let me see it. . . ." Thane took the box, forced the thin tip of the screwdriver blade into the gap between lid and body, close to the keyhole, and gave a sharp twist. The lock smashed, the lid flew open.

"This is what we wanted." The box space was almost filled. First, there were several bundles of crisp, obviously new five-pound notes. Beneath them was a long brown envelope, bulky and heavily sealed. Putting the money aside, Thane ripped open the envelope and with almost loving care drew out a thick bundle of car registration books. Together, they examined the documents. All referred to cars first registered within the previous six months. The names and addresses varied, as did the dates of registration. The two newest books had been issued within the previous ten days.

"Erick Millan's stock in trade," said Thane, prodding the fanned-out bundle. "These had to lie here maturing until they'd aged enough to be used. If this little bundle got out—how many are there, anyway?"

"Thirty-four—thirty-five, thirty-six." Moss finished the count. "Not all Glasgow-issued either. At least four different county authorities are in that bunch."

Thane gathered the registration books together again. "Well, the important thing is we've got them now. Before we're finished, we'll have to ask the Taxation Department for a complete check on all Ascension registration requests and sort out the fake from the genuine. That's going to be hell's own delight for someone"—there was a tap at the door—"come in!"

The door opened, and Sergeant MacLeod herded a small procession into the room. Puggy Carson was first, his left wrist handcuffed to Jacko Menran's right. Menran's other wrist was similarly manacled to Liscomb's right. They shuffled awkwardly forward—the car thief, the fixer, and the seller, each knowing his luck had run out, each with his own attitude to what lay ahead. Halted in front of the desk, Sergeant MacLeod and another C.I.D. man behind them, their attitudes were in considerable contrast. Puggy Carson was relaxed, almost friendly as he glanced around the room. But at the other end of the line, Liscomb was sallow and trembling—while, between them, handcuff links jingling, Jacko Menran was openly hostile.

Thane looked them over. "Let's not waste time on this," he said in a hard, flat voice. "We've got enough evidence against each of you to get a conviction in any court, no matter how you wriggle." He slapped the registration books down before him. "We've also got these, we've traced back some of the cars from the Bacarro showroom, and we know exactly how the setup was working. If it helps, you've been under constant observation for the past day or so."

"But what about Millan—" Liscomb edged forward, dry-lipped, in a near panic. "He—"

"Keep your mouth shut, you fool," growled Menran, turning on his companion. "They're hoping we'll start talking—why make it easy for them?"

Liscomb found support from an unexpected quarter.

"Doesn't seem much sense to me in keeping quiet," shrugged Puggy Carson. "Look, Chief Inspector, when your boys picked me up you said something I didn't like, I didn't like at all. You said there was a murder rap involved in this. Right?"

"There still is," said Thane, leaning back in his chair, arms folded, watching the car thief's crumpled face.

"Uh-huh." Puggy turned to his two companions. "Now you blokes can do what you like, see? But I'm wriggling out from under anything with that kind of label on it. This is pal Erick's room—but where is he, eh? And where's Ben MacGhee, come to that?"

Menran scowled, his eyes fixed floorwards. But Liscomb stuttered in his eagerness to agree. "That's wha-what I w-wanted to say, Chief Inspector. Wh-where's Erick Millan? It's all his affair, this whole bu-business."

"That's a load of tripe for a start," said Puggy cheerfully. "You've got us cold to rights, Mr. Thane, no sense in mucking about. All right, I've done time before . . . so now I do another spell, maybe short, maybe long. Should I break my heart?" He grinned. "If you want some help, well, mutual co-operation's my middle name today."

"No deals." Thane extinguished the car thief's hopeful hint with an ice-cold frown. "I'll tell you this much. Mac-Ghee's dead and Millan's on the run."

The last vestiges of colour drained from Liscomb's face. Even Menran looked up, mouth half-open as if about to speak. Then his lips clamped tight again. Puggy was first to recover. "Who did for Ben?"

Phil Moss answered that one, unwrapping a bismuth tablet and putting it into his mouth as he spoke. "Erick Millan— didn't you know?"

"Us?" Puggy Carson's eyes were wide with surprise. "Hell, no—"

"You saw Erick Millan yesterday when you took that stolen Austin from Menran's place to the Bacarro showrooms," snapped Thane. "Had he quarrelled with MacGhee before then?"

"No—" Carson was openly bewildered. "He said Mac-Ghee had gone a bit soft, but that he was—" The car thief stopped short, suddenly wary.

"Go on," said Thane, leaning forward. "This isn't a game we're playing, Carson."

"H-he said he had fixed it so MacGhee would take care of Old Ludd Millan," volunteered Liscomb eagerly. "That's what it was, Chief Inspector. His uncle h-had been snooping around and Erick said they'd have to have another accident."

Carson nodded agreement. "That's right, Chief Inspector."

"What did you think that meant?" Thane waited.

"Well—" Carson licked his lips. "I suppose I took it he'd put the old man out of the road, same as he did for Sammy Bell."

Thane frowned. "Erick Millan didn't kill Bell. His uncle's admitted doing that, Carson . . . better try again."

The car thief needed a moment or two to digest that piece of information. "The basket . . . look, I was levelling with you. We thought it was an accident, like the papers said. Then Erick starts dropping hints that Sammy got his because he was creating trouble. You mean . . . he probably thought it was an accident too, and was faking up the story to scare us into line? He hinted he did it all right . . . didn't he, Jacko?"

Menran gave a sullen nod of agreement. "Maybe Mac-Ghee wanted to back out—he always was too soft for the setup."

Thane had only a few more questions remaining. Menran still bitterly obstructive, the other two almost competing in their answers, he learned that Sammy Bell's role in the gang had been threefold. In addition to acting with Carson in the actual thefts, he'd used the Ascension filling station's repair shop as a late-night halfway house for several of the

stolen cars—and also as a place where car "guarantee" repairs were quietly carried out on the side for Bacarro
Motors' customers. The showroom had no repair facilities
of its own.

When Sammy Bell died, they'd had no real worries over
the possibility of his having left anything behind which
might implicate them.

"Sammy knew the ropes," growled Menran. "He took no
chances. Besides, Erick said he was there when you were,
and that you found nothing."

But it was less fruitful when Thane turned to Millan's
possible hiding place.

"I'd tell you if I knew, so help me," declared Puggy
Carson. "But Millan wasn't the type who thought about
getting caught—I know." He gave a soft curse. "Trying to
scare the daylights out of us . . . the basket."

"All right, that's the lot for now," said Thane with curt
finality. "Sergeant—book 'em in for me."

Sergeant MacLeod gave a firm tug on Carson's free arm,
and the handcuffed trio were led out.

"Ironic, isn't it?" Phil Moss patted his pockets in search
of a cigarette, then took one from the packet extended by
Thane. He struck a match, and they smoked in silence for
a moment. "Old Ludd kills Bell to keep young Erick in the
clear—and the little swine, though he thinks it's an accident
himself, uses Bell's death to keep his own mob in line. A
filthy setup."

"Aye." Thane gave a growl of agreement, and rose from
behind the desk. "Ludd Millan's going to find out sooner
or later that his beloved nephew was worth even less than
what little he still imagines. Erick probably killed Mac-
Ghee just because the poor devil wouldn't help him murder
Old Ludd. Come on, we've a lot of people to see—just about
everyone who was a friend of Erick Millan."

He stopped, the door half-opened. "It's a long time since I disliked anyone quite as much as this glamour-boy, Phil. It's going to be a pleasure, a real pleasure, to see him in the dock."

By three P.M. Erick Millan had been at liberty for over five hours—and for the Millside team, that represented a period of nonstop activity. One by one, Millan's friends in the city were being visited, questioned, and eliminated. Most wanted to be helpful, once they accepted the initial shock that the racing driver was now a fugitive. A few suggested places where he might have gone to earth . . . and each location was checked out in turn.

But Erick Millan had left little trace of his movements after that cross-roof dash from the Ascension garage. Only one report of any value reached Thane as the C.I.D. cars continued their constant journeying. A pedal cycle had been stolen from a spot close by the garage. It had been found abandoned near the centre of the city.

Newspaper pressure grew, until at last, a bleak-faced pipe-puffing Chief Superintendent by his side, Thane was forced to hold a brief press conference. A score of reporters crammed into the C.I.D. room, and gave a joint rumble of disappointment at the end of his short, cautiously worded statement.

Jock Mills of the *Bugle* stood quietly at the rear as a fat, red-faced pressman declared: "There must be more than this, Chief Inspector. You say that 'following a visit by officers of Millside Division to the head office of Ascension Motors, and other action taken in the city, four men are in custody.' All right—we know that, and we know you took a dead man from the garage. How about Erick Millan, eh? You've got a special search out for him. What's going on?"

Impassively, Thane glanced down at the written statement in his hand. "I told you four men will appear in court
tomorrow. I've also told you that a fifth man is wanted for
questioning. If you put two and two together and make
four, that's your business. You all know dam' well how the
law ties me down on what I can say once we've got men
on a charge. Wait until tomorrow's court if you want more
—and just remember that if your arithmetic means that
two and two make five, then you and your editor may both
end up on a contempt of court charge. Good day, gentlemen."

Grumbling, the pressmen filed out. The Scottish courts
were sensitive on the subject of newspaper reports which
gave too much detail at a time when arrests were in progress. They accepted the situation in the same way in which
they accepted Thane's reasons for sticking to his skeletal
statement—but that didn't mean they were happy about
either position.

As the last man vanished, Ilford removed the pipe from
his mouth. "Well, that's given them something to chew over.
What's next on your list?"

Thane rubbed one weary hand across the back of his
neck. "I'd say Millan's now well out of the city or we'd
have had some trace of him. If he's outside, sir, then he
could be pretty well anywhere—north, south, east, west, we
can pretty well take our choice."

"Tried pumping the uncle?"

"Old Ludd? Yes. No help there. As far as I can make out,
he knows very little about what Erick's been up to over the
past few years."

"Any other ideas?" Ilford rose, the pipe going back in
his mouth. He didn't wait for an answer. "Keep trying,
Colin—and keep in touch." The burly figure padded from
the room. Moments after he'd gone, Phil Moss entered

carrying a tin-lid tray with two mugs of tea and a plate of sandwiches.

"Food." He set the tray on the desk. "Remember when we had some last? About seven A.M.—and my ulcer's whining."

Thane talked as he ate. "Phil, there's one person we haven't got round to yet. . . . I'm leaving you in charge here while I go out to see her."

"Her?" Moss raised an eyebrow. "You mean . . ."

"A certain Chief Constable's daughter," agreed Thane. He reached out for another sandwich.

The house was almost an hour away from the city by car, a big two-storey mansion standing in its own grounds, every line of its grey stone showing mellowed age and careful maintenance.

Inside, in the lounge, Thane sat with his back to the broad French windows, opened wide and giving a view of the sun-lit garden beyond. County Chief Constables, he reflected, obviously led a pleasant life.

"Coffee, Mr. Thane?" The slim brunette before him still managed to appear as well-shaped in a tweed costume as she had been in the white cocktail dress of the newspaper photograph. She poured from the silver pot, then handed him the tiny cup and saucer. "Help yourself to sugar." She poured a second cup for herself, then sat down in the arm-chair opposite.

"I'm sorry to disturb you like this . . ." the words sounded awkward, and he knew it. "But as I said when I phoned, we need help, help you may be able to give us."

The girl sipped her coffee. "I know most of what's happened, of course. My father phoned me this morning from County Headquarters." She saw the surprise on Thane's face, and smiled. "I think you should understand, Chief Inspector, that my father trusts me. He said that if Erick Millan tried to contact me I was to let him know immediately—that was just after the Glasgow 'special search' request went out."

"And has Millan tried?"

She shook her head. "No—he might have, but he hasn't so far." The girl lifted the silver box by her side, and opened it. "Cigarette? I don't smoke myself—but these are Father's." She waited until he had it lit, then went on. "Maybe it would make things easier for you if I put my emotional situation on the record. I like Erick Millan—perhaps I should say 'liked,' I don't know. I met him at a party a few months back. Since then we've gone around a lot together—the last time was a few days ago."

"Last Thursday," prompted Thane.

Her eyes twinkled. "I wondered about that reporter—his interview makes sense now. Anyway, I've no illusions about Erick's love-life. Good-looking girls are part of the Millan circus—some more than others. But Erick was too fond of the gay life to tie himself down, and I knew it. Satisfied?"

Thane nodded. "Then I've only one question to ask you. If he hasn't contacted you, have you any idea where he might be? Take it that he's got out of Glasgow—we're pretty sure of that by now. He's on the run, and desperate. He's a man who knows he's pretty well bound to be recognised if he stays in one spot for any length of time. Knowing him, where do you think he'd head for?"

The girl frowned. "I'd an idea that was why you were coming out. You know what I think he'll try to do? Lie low somewhere for a few days until he grows a moustache or even a beard, maybe even dye his hair, and give the—the 'heat' you call it, isn't it?—time to wear off a little."

"That could make sense," agreed Thane, suddenly hopeful.

"And there is one place, a place where he knows he'd find food and shelter—and almost a cast-iron guarantee of being left alone until at least the end of the week.

"Ever gone skiing, Chief Inspector?"

"No."

"Erick has. He took me north about six weeks ago. Half a dozen of us went up to the Cairngorms for a week end. There are plenty of good ski-runs in the mountains around Aviemore."

"And you think he's heading for there?"

She poured more coffee. "When we were up there, we became tired skiing after a while and stopped for a rest. The view was magnificent—we were fairly high up—and one of the other couples with us had spent a climbing holiday in the area. They began naming all the different peaks around. There's one big mountain called Ben Macdhui.

"I remember their telling us about some little rescue huts on it—they're tiny little things, high up, intended for climbers who land in trouble. There's food and blankets and other stuff there, with everyone on their honour not to use the place except in an emergency."

Thane rose to his feet. "It's the nearest thing to a lead we've had yet. Would Millan know the exact location of these huts?"

"I think so—we were pretty interested in them at the time." The girl got up to show him out. "What do you do now?"

"Get back to Millside and find out some more about your mountain," said Thane briskly. "Thank you—and tell your father I'm sorry I didn't have time to call round at his office."

She laughed. "Daddy? When I told him you were coming he was all for being here—counsel for the defence or something. I told him to stay where he was and mind his own business."

It appeared that even a Chief Constable could be henpecked. Thane headed for the waiting car.

By nine P.M. Erick Millan had been at liberty for almost twelve hours. In Thane's office, a slowly mounting pile of cigarette butts in the big glass ash tray were as effective as any other measure of time. In one corner of the room Phil Moss made a half-hearted attempt to read a paperback Western. At his desk, Thane found himself staring at the telephone, willing it to ring. Until it did, with news one way or the other, they were helpless. In the city and beyond, other men were continuing the monotonous routine of search and watch—but the two Millside men had their hopes nailed to the high, snow-capped mountain of granite rock called Macdhui.

An orderly came and went, bringing fresh coffee and a sheaf of routine teleprinter messages—an armed robbery in Edinburgh, four young thugs escaped from a Borstal detention centre in Stirlingshire, look-out requested for a green two-ton van loaded with cloth stolen from Ayr—the messages could vary, the theme remained constant.

The telephone rang at ten minutes past nine. The two men looked at each other and, with a flaring sense of promise, Thane snatched up the receiver, Phil Moss already over by his side.

"Thane. . . ."

"Detective Inspector Buchan, Inverness County Headquarters." The quiet Highland voice came clear over the distance. "Sorry to have been so long, but there's a lot of ground to cover up around here—our lads had to check around the local youth hostels and climbing hotels, and that means waiting until the last of the folk have come down from the hills."

"That's all right." Thane tried to keep on the same calm level as the Inverness man. "Any luck?"

"Aye." There was almost a chuckle in the word. "I think you're in luck, man. A team of climbers who were coming back down towards the Lairig Ghru—that's the main pass from the mountains—saw a man going out the way on his own. They thought it strange, like. It lacked only a couple of hours or so till darkness, and most folk would be heading back towards base, not starting out. But they watched him for a bit, and he seemed to know what he was doing . . . they decided he must have a camp further up."

"Could they describe him?"

"After a fashion. One of the fellows put the binoculars on him. He was a good bit away, mind, but from what they say it sounds awful like yon Millan."

"Any word on how he could have got up?" probed Thane.

"Well, that's not quite so clear," admitted the county officer. "If he's your man he obviously got past the Glasgow road blocks for a start." Point made and taken, he went on. "Aviemore's a wee place, but one that's used to plenty of strangers passing through—the hikers and the holidaymakers as well as those heading for the mountain. He didn't come by the bus or train, that we know. I'd say he probably got a lift along the way from some lorryman. Now, Chief Inspector, will you be coming up?"

"We will," agreed Thane grimly.

"Good. There's not a thing we can do until daylight anyway—nobody in their right mind would start heading up Ben Macdhui way in the darkness, not if they ever wanted to come down again, anyway. If you come up by the train, now, I'll have a car meet you at Aviemore. How many of you will there be?"

"If you can lay on a couple of your men who know the area, then there will be just two of us—D.I. Moss and myself."

"That'll be arranged—and a good journey." The line went dead as the other man hung up.

The overnight sleeper train from Glasgow's Buchanan Street left at 11.15 P.M. They caught it with time to spare, and the two men slept sound in their berths as the train

rumbled north past Perth to Pitlochry, red glow from its
fire-box piercing the cloaking darkness as it huffed on
through the wild, wooded gash of the Pass of Killiecrankie,
climbing high through Glen Garry, then running more
smoothly on the long slow descent beyond.

At 4.10 A.M. the train pulled to a halt at Aviemore's tiny
station, steam hissing restlessly. Thane and Moss were the
only two passengers to alight, and within a few seconds
the long line of coaches glided out again, carrying their
sleeping occupants on to Inverness and journey's end.

The two men blinked sleepily as they stood in the station's
gloom. There was a solitary porter in sight, and then another figure, broad-built, dressed in old tweed trousers, a
grey anorak climbing blouse worn loose over a heavy wool
sweater, came along the platform towards them.

"Mr. Thane?" the man gave a half-salute. "I'm Sergeant
MacNeil—D.I. Buchan asked me to meet you. The car's
outside." They shook hands, and followed him out of the
station to where the police car waited, sidelights bright
in the darkness.

Another man was waiting by the car, similarly clad.
"Constable Stewart," introduced MacNeil. "I know the parts
around here pretty well, but Donny was born and raised
among these rocks. He's as good a guide as you'll find."

Stewart grinned a greeting. "Och, well, I'll chust be trying not to get you lost, anyway," he agreed.

They got into the car.

"There's about half an hour lacking till sunrise," said
Sergeant MacNeil. "Donny and I thought you might be
wanting to start off now to where we'll have to leave the
car and go on on foot. We've got a bit breakfast with us—
and some boots and kit that should fit you."

"Boots?" Phil Moss raised a querulous eyebrow.

"Aye." The two County men exchanged a faint smile, and
MacNeil added, "It's a wee bit rough where we're going,

Inspector. You wouldn't get far in your city shoes, and you wouldn't be wanting to. Have either of you done any climbing before?"

"Not me." Moss shook his head.

"You, sir?"

Thane grimaced. "About fifteen years ago, but not since."

"Mmh. Och, well, most of it iss really walking uphill, the way we will be going," said Constable Stewart consolingly. He started the engine, and the car purred to life. They drove through the darkened, silent village, then, headlights blazing, turned off on to a narrower road, a twisting winding route which gradually became more rough in character. They turned off again on to a still smaller pathway, car springs jerking over the occasional pothole, and finally, as the sky above began to show the first grey traces of coming dawn, the car came to a halt just short of where the road ended.

"We'll eat first, I think," declared MacNeil, switching on the interior light and glancing at his watch. "We can be on our way by five o'clock." The two Inverness men produced flasks, plastic cups, and a paper-wrapped bundle of sandwiches and proceeded to share them out.

As they ate, the sky continued to lighten, towering grey half-shapes began to form ahead, and finally, as the soft dawn gave way to harsh daylight, the mountains loomed above them—an apparently unending vista of lofty, flat-topped peaks, green slopes giving way to the first speckled patches of purple heather, then above, and beyond, bleak, glowering granite rock, black where the deep hollowed corries cast their shadows close to the first sprinklings of white, advance guard of the snow line above. The Cairngorm Mountains, Scotland's highest continuous area of ground over the 4000-foot mark, lay waiting.

Sergeant MacNeil swirled the last dregs of coffee from his cup on to the grass, and pointed. "That one's the Cairngorm itself—but the higher one, to the right and beyond, sir, that's where we're heading." He chuckled. "Aye, it's a black-looking brute—but it's no'too bad if you know the ways. Leastwise, Queen Victoria managed to climb it when she was a lassie, so I reckon we'll manage."

Phil Moss had certain doubts. But while MacNeil went round to the car boot and began dragging out an impressive quantity of equipment, he asked the other County man, "How far up do we have to go?"

Donny Stewart, his lanky frame sprawled on the dew-moist grass, pondered the position. "Ach, it is not too bad," he declared. "The Macdhui is the second highest mountain in all Scotland—they used to be thinking it wass the highest, until someone discovered they'd chust made a bit mistake. But we don't haff to be going to the top, Inspector, and anyway, it is late spring—the snow and ice hass gone well back."

"Just where are we heading, anyway?" demanded Thane, as MacNeil dumped a selection of boots and clothing before them.

While the two C.I.D. men struggled into the unfamiliar mountain equipment, Donny Stewart used a broken twig to trace their route.

"We're here now—at Glenmore," he explained. "Our way iss through the trees there, to the Lairig Ghru, that gap you see between the two wee bit hills."

Changing into a pair of brown corduroys and a wool sweater which was the twin of MacNeil's, Thane glanced up at the "wee bit hills" and gauged them each considerably over the 2000-foot mark.

"Don't be worrying about that stretch, or going up the Ghru," said Donny. "It iss a rough walk, but little more. From there, we go round the north side on Ben Macdhui itself. I'm thinking there is only one likely place for your man to be—and that is not by the ski slopes, or the popular climbs."

Sergeant MacNeil nodded agreement. "As we see it, sir, Millan would steer clear of the main areas where there might be occasional folk about. The mountains are pretty quiet at this time—it's midway between the skiing and the summer climbing—but there's always one or two parties out. Donny and I think he's more likely to be on the quiet side of the Ben. The place is just as wild, but the climbing isn't spectacular enough for the mountaineers . . . and there's a wee rescue shelter up there, close by the snow line.

"We'll start when you're ready, sir."

"These are too big," complained Moss, contemplating the heavy clinker-nailed boots before him.

"Try another pair of socks to fill out the space," advised MacNeil, shouldering a long coil of nylon rope. Donny Stewart swung a well-filled rucksack on his back, then paused, a faint doubt crossing his face.

"This man Millan, sir—iss he likely to be difficult?"

"I'm pretty sure he's not armed, if that's what you mean," said Thane. "For the rest, we'll need to wait and find out."

"Chust so, chust so." Donny gave a grunt of satisfaction as Phil Moss declared himself satisfied with the sock-padded boots. Then he set off, leading the way with a smooth, deceptively easygoing stride which was close to a lope. Thane came next, followed by Moss, with Sergeant Mac-Neil at the rear.

An hour later, halfway up the Lairig Ghru, they were allowed a brief rest. Ben Macdhui was nearer now, its highest reaches wisped by cloud, the challenging lines of its rock buttresses throwing an occasional brilliant sparkle of light as the sun glanced mirrorlike from some quartz outcrop. Five minutes, no more, he allowed them before they set off again, climbing higher now, grass giving way to heather and rock. Once Donny suddenly held up his hand—

and they froze, while a small herd of deer, led by a majestic stag, moved slowly across a nearby slope. There were birds, not many but frequent enough for them to become used to the sudden whirr of wings as grouse or ptarmigan darted skywards from some hidden hollow. Behind them, the low grasslands seemed shrunk to almost toyland proportions. Ahead, the going became rougher as their guide swung them off the path and began to strike west. Boot soles scraped more frequently on rock—and even MacNeil seemed pleased when they took another brief break by a tiny, silver-clear burn, its water snow-cool from the mountaintop above.

Donny drove them on. The granite boulders were growing large now, occasionally they threaded their way along the side of a sheer rock face, and the first white traces of snow told its own story of height.

"Nearing three thousand feet now," said Donny laconically. "Chust be keeping an eye open, chentlemen—there sometimes can be the big stone falling down. That iss all a mountain really iss, you know . . . a great big piece of stone, with little bits starting to fall off."

Plodding on, forehead beaded in sweated exertion, Thane was conscious of one thing above all else—the clean, quiet, almost unnatural silence into which they were moving, a silence broken only by the occasional crunch of boot on rock. Suddenly even that noise was muffled as they were enveloped by a swirl of soft, eddying mist.

"Chust keep close together now," advised Donny. "There's not much of this. We go straight on . . ." the world had become cold, claustrophobic grey as the mist cloud closed thick around them.

Thane looked ahead . . . then felt the hairs on his neck prickle. Before them, indistinct in the mist, loomed a huge shadowy figure—man-shaped, but giant. Behind him, he heard Moss give a sudden gasp. Then, almost as quickly, the shadow vanished.

"The Grey Man," said MacNeil, his voice almost a whisper. "You saw it, Donny?"

"Aye." Their guide's voice was solemn. "Only once before haff I seen him, and that long years ago."

"What the devil was it?" Thane recovered from the surprise.

"We call it the Grey Man of the Cairngorms," said Donny. "Och, the experts will tell you it iss chust your own reflection thrown back by the mist and the sun—like they say there's no monster in Loch Ness."

"It gave me a hell of a turn, anyway," gasped Moss. Glad of the unexpected rest, he leaned back against a handy rock.

"And many another poor soul too, Inspector." Donny squared his thin shoulders. "We must move on now . . . there iss not so terrible far left to go."

"Donny—what do you think the Grey Man is?" Thane eased his cramped shoulder muscles.

"Me, sir?" Donny shook his head. "I am chust a dam' stupid Highland polisman whose grandmother told him too many fey tales—too many by far, whateffer." He began to stride off, the others stumbling to follow before he disappeared into the mist.

Ten minutes later they were clear again, moving crabwise along the side of a steep-sloping wilderness of broken rock. Here and there, a tuft of heather forced a weak growth from some narrow crack. The rest was bare granite desolation.

"Nearly there now, sir," said Sergeant MacNeil. "We cross this slope, go up a gully and the shelter hut's on ahead."

Thane looked up and around. "That means a direct approach."

"It does, sir—but there's no—" MacNeil broke off, his

mouth half-open, gazing up the slope. "Falling stone!" he exclaimed.

"In here, quick. . . ." Donny dragged them behind a giant fist-shaped outcrop of granite as, rumbling and crashing, the boulder swept down from above, smashing a path through lesser obstacles, bouncing as it glanced off sturdier slabs. A small avalanche of lesser debris trailing in its wake, it thundered past.

Donny Stewart drew the sleeve of his anorak across his forehead. "Some things are meant as a warning," he muttered. Then, more cheerfully, "We can be going on now."

Warily, he stepped from their cover and the others followed, slithering on hands and knees. It still wasn't climbing in mountaineer's language, but it was tough enough going for any man to wish.

Thirty yards on . . . and another rumble began. Above, another mass of granite several hundredweights, began its steam-rolling path downwards, gaining momentum at a frightening rate. Donny glanced desperately around, then with a shout and a wave urged them downwards. The four men slid and scrambled after him and dropped into their only cover—a ridged crevice in the rock surface. Bellies down, they waited the long, agonising seconds while the thunder grew louder. Then a shower of small stones sprayed around them as the granite boulder, black against the sky, hurtled over and past them.

"He's maybe no' armed, sir," said MacNeil quietly. "But these rocks make a hell of a good substitute for artillery."

"Millan?"

Donny nodded agreement. "Aye, I saw it too, sergeant. There was a man up there, Chief Inspector—and it does not take such an awful big shove to start one of these dam' great boulders on its way."

In direct confirmation, another rumble began above. The rock crevice seemed to vibrate—and then that boulder too had gone past, crashing on its downward path, running to the left of their makeshift shelter.

Levering himself to a crouch, Thane peered upwards. The granite-strewn slope seemed deserted—but somewhere up there Millan was lurking, another jagged missile ready and waiting, and plenty more near to hand, ready to follow behind. A direct rush up that slope would be little more than a tragic farce, two, maybe three hundreds yards of a steep toiling ascent in the face of a bombardment of deadly stone moving down on them at a speed of many yards per second.

"We need better cover," he growled. "Then we've got to find another way up—one where we won't feel like pins in a bowling alley."

"Aye, indeed, you have the right way of it," agreed Donny slowly. He eased the rucksack from his back. "We'll be haffing to move fast, though. If we can get from here to thon big rock over on the right—aye, the one shaped like an old man's head, and him weary—we'll be safer. And there iss a wee bit gully from there—"

Thane measured the distance, a full forty yards across the stony slope, but at a slightly downward angle. "Let's go, then . . . but one at a time."

The others understood the hidden meaning, and gave brief nods of agreement.

Sergeant MacNeil went first, diving from cover, crouching close to the surface, boot nails rasping while the others waited for the first rumble from above. But MacNeil skidded to a halt behind the head-shaped rock and gave a triumphant thumbs-up sign. Phil Moss followed, jerky, less footsure in the heavy, unaccustomed boots but still moving fast.

He was fifteen yards out when the boulder began to move . . . a slow topple at first, then that sudden downhill acceleration. Moss gave a despairing glance and redoubled his efforts, moving almost on hands and knees. Two-thirds across, his feet slipped, and he fell. Thane groaned aloud as the giant granite rock bounced high from a projecting spur and sped towards the once again frantically moving man. He heard a sudden cry—then Phil seemed to disappear as the boulder swept down in a rush of accompanying fragments.

He and Donny were out of the crevice almost simultaneously, heading towards the crumpled figure. As they neared him, another rock began to roll—but, grasping an arm each, they dragged Moss to safety, Sergeant MacNeil helping to bundle them into shelter as the boulder thundered past.

They laid Moss down, his head pillowed in a folded anorak. He was unconscious, a long gash high on his forehead.

"Left leg's broken too," said MacNeil, examining him with a surprisingly gentle touch. "He caught a load from these smaller stones, but the big fellow missed him—or he'd be smeared halfway down the mountain by now." He frowned. "The cut on the head's not serious—he'll be coming round in a minute or so. But I could do with having something to splint this leg. I can strap it up a bit, that's all."

Donny burrowed into one of his deep, bulging pockets and produced a tiny flask. "A wee sensation of whisky will help him," he suggested, passing it over. "Well, Chief Inspector, what now? We could move your friend to the rescue hut—it iss not far, and the way iss safe. One of us could be going for help, too."

Reluctantly, Thane shook his head. "That way, Millan would see us go and could make another break for it. We might take days to catch up with him again. You said there's a route from here that would take us above him."

"Aye, but it's not one for carrying a man with a broken leg."

"All right— Sergeant, you stay here with Inspector Moss, and keep showing yourself from time to time. Just enough to keep Millan occupied, right?" He turned to the other county officer. "Donny, I want you to get me up above Millan. After that, you head back down towards Aviemore as if that Grey Man of yours was hard at your heels—and get back here as fast as possible with a stretcher party."

The policeman guide's eyes narrowed. "And why would I be leaving you alone up there to tackle that black-hearted piece of Lowland scum?" he objected.

"Because there's no other way," said Thane softly. "I'm not going to pull rank on you, laddie—but that's the way it's going to be."

They tried one brief experiment before they set out. Thane crawled a few slow yards from the shelter of their rock—then came back twice as quickly as a boulder began to dance downhill. Erick Millan was still up there, ready and waiting.

Donny stopped just long enough to have a brief, murmured conversation with his sergeant and to collect the coil of nylon rope. Then, their movements hidden from above by the overhanging rock, he and Thane slid downhill, dropped into the gully trench, and set off.

High up on the crest of the slope, Erick Millan crouched in the lee of a jumble of broken rock and peered down to the spot where his pursuers lay waiting. They were close enough now for there to be no need of the binoculars by his side— the binoculars through which he had first seen them a long way off as they toiled towards him.

He tensed, hands widespread against the cold stone of yet another boulder, as a figure emerged for a few brief seconds. Then, as the man below ducked back into cover again, he relaxed once more. No, they weren't so keen to come out now—not since one of them had been hit. It had been Moss, he was pretty sure . . . certainly Thane was

still on his feet. Millan gave a cold chuckle as he recalled
how the Chief Inspector had skipped back to safety as that
last rock had gone crashing down.

A shiver of cold went through him. The snow line was
close, and the chill morning temperature reflected its near-
ness. The north side of the Ben, with its dark corries where
the sun seldom penetrated, had reaches covered ten feet
deep in perpetual white—brick-hard snow which might
soften a little in midsummer days, but which quickly froze
again by night. He wished he'd brought one of the blankets
from the hut, or even some of the iron ration chocolate
he'd found among the other food supplies.

If only he'd had a gun, too—the revolver Old Ludd had
used to club down the cop in his office back at the Ascension
garage. . . .

Rumpled, unshaven, Erick Millan felt a lifetime away
from that surprise moment when, the detective suddenly
slumped on the floor, Old Ludd had waved him towards
the window. He hadn't stopped to ask why, either. Old
Ludd wouldn't hand over the revolver, and with Thane
prowling the workshop floor, certain to find Ben MacGhee's
body at any moment, the racing driver had decided there
was no time to waste.

"Thane—" he glared down the mountain slope, snarled
the word aloud, and cursed the big Chief Inspector.

If Thane hadn't pulled the raid that morning there might
have been a chance of his getting away with MacGhee's
death as just another accident.

MacGhee had had to die. He remembered the man's
whining declaration, "I won't do it, Erick—I'm not getting
myself involved in murder, not even for the sake of the
cars." Yet why not? He'd worked out a simple enough plan
to dispose of his uncle once and for all. There was little or
no risk for MacGhee in the scheme, either. Just bring Old
Ludd over to the inspection pit where the lorry waited,

then have that gearbox "slip" when the man was underneath. MacGhee had sealed his own fate, however, when he'd said that he was through, finished—that he was going to spill the whole truth about Bacarro Motors to Old Ludd first thing the next morning.

Millan's lips twisted mirthlessly. He'd killed MacGhee then, once he'd seen that the special magic of those racing engines had at last worn thin. And what was to have been a trap for Old Ludd had become a ready-made accident scene for the mechanic's body.

There was more movement below. "Oh, no you don't . . ." with a grunt, he heaved forward on the granite boulder, then, as it began to tilt, gave a final exertion. The rock began trundling, faster and faster—and the figure below vanished back to cover before its oncoming menace.

Thane . . . he could only have tracked him to up here through the girl. How long had he been working on the case anyway—how long since he'd first found a link between the hot car trade and Erick Millan, the racing hero? It could have been through Sammy Bell, or earlier.

"What the hell, anyway?" he muttered.

Thane was down there, he was up above, and for the moment his personal ambition was restricted to having the chance to see several hundredweights of stone make contact with the detective. At least he'd got this far. Once clear of the garage there had been the pedal cycle into town, then a walk around the quiet back streets while he decided his next move. That had been to climb on a local-stop bus, heading out towards the Stirling road. He'd got off again well before the city boundary. After that, it had simply been a case of walking—funny, in a mechanised age a man walking along a road had become so innocent as to be almost insignificant. He'd walked round the road blocks. The East Germans had shown that—you could watch a city's main roads, but to seal off every lane and footpath required a full-scale military operation. Besides, Erick Millan hoofing it was probably the last thing the police would have thought of. There wasn't much more—a bus journey to Perth, hidden behind the pair of sun glasses he had bought at a roadside shop. More purchases there—boots, a sweater, the binoculars, a pair of Government surplus army trousers—and then the hitchhiking journey north, a somewhat down-at-heel climber on his way to the mountains.

And now? Millan shrugged, and concentrated on the slope below.

More than anything else, Colin Thane wanted to rest— to relax for a few brief, precious seconds. At that moment, it was the last thing he could do.

Once they'd dropped into the shallow gully, Donny had kept up a cracking pace. They'd scrambled along its length, turned the corner of a high rock buttress and then, stopping at its base, the county man pointed straight upwards.

"He canna see us here, sir—and that's the way we're going. There iss only one other route, and it would take a couple of hours longer."

So they went straight up. The rock chimney was wide enough at first to be tackled in a straight-forward way, one Thane remembered from the many years ago when he'd last tried it. Back hard against one wall, feet against the other, body in a right-angle position, moving upwards was a simple though strenuous business of raising feet and back alternately, hands pressed against the rock to ease the upward movement. Donny was on ahead, the nylon line linking them, giving Thane a feeling of much-needed security.

Halfway up, there was a chockstone—several tons of granite boulder sitting like an ungainly stopper in a rough-hewn bottle. Donny got them over that by a piece of hair-raising rock-climbing where for long, horrifying seconds both their lives hung on the strength of his fingers. If he'd fallen, Thane would have been hauled after him. Instead, Donny surmounted the chockstone, hauled Thane up beside him and showed him their final stretch.

They had to leave the main chimney now, and tackle a much narrower, yet in some ways less treacherous distance. The crack, a narrow fissure wide enough to admit an arm and a leg, but no more, rippled upwards for some fifty feet.

"Chust take your time on it now, sir," advised Donny. "If you get into trouble, all there iss to do iss to hug that rock as if your life depended on it."

Gazing upwards, Thane decided it probably would.

They started. At times the fissure narrowed suddenly, so that, fingers gripping on one hold, a booted foot had to be wedged across the walls of the crack to give sufficient leverage for the next move.

On ahead, Donny seemed to have few awkward moments. For Thane, their progress seemed snail-like, the time when he had to resort to a hand-jam, clenched fist wedged upright against the cold grey enmity of the rock, an enduring nightmare, the gentle upward drag of the nylon rope assuming paramount importance.

Then the drag of the rope became a supporting pull as, boots scraping, Donny reached the top. A few moments later, Thane was beside him, lying gasping for breath, muscles quivering a concerted protest against unaccustomed strain.

Ahead, the mountain rose gently for about twenty feet to the edge of a ridge. Donny coiled the rope, draped it over his shoulder, and gave a cheerful grin. "Well, we made it—though I wass in two minds about that for a wee spell. Now, sir, I'll be going away back down. Chust you crawl quiet-like up to the ridge there, and you'll haff the grandest view." With a brief wave of farewell, he lowered himself back into the crack and disappeared from view.

Thane lay still, waiting till his breathing slowed to near normal and his heart beat seemed back to its usual pace. He looked over the edge, down the length of the crack, saw Donny making sure and steady progress towards the chockstone, then crawled towards the ridge. Cautiously, he raised his head and peeped over.

Two hundred feet away, down a smooth, gentle slope, Erick Millan crouched low, eyes still fixed down the steep length beyond, oblivious of the man now stalking behind him.

Two hundred feet, and no intervening cover. To the left, the slope continued, lost from sight as it turned beneath a bold-fronted crag.

It was time Millan received some payment in his own coin. Edging back, Thane carefully selected a smooth, rounded granite stone, twice the size of a football, and pushed and dragged its weight to the lip of the ridge. Now—he shoved it over, and as the boulder began bouncing he was on his feet, following it at the run. It travelled fast, soft-sounding for a moment then growling along a path towards its target.

The sudden noise, nerve-jangling in the mountain silence, brought Millan spinning round. He appeared hypnotised by the sight of the danger rushing towards him and the figure charging close behind. Then, just in time, he jumped clear. The stone smashed into the rock debris, spun high, then went rumbling on.

Shaken, Millan lost precious seconds before he turned and ran to the left, his speed desperate along the rock-jumbled slope, Thane less than a hundred feet behind him. Pounding on, the faint downward gradient of the curving route now his only ally, he felt the salt taste of sweat on his lips, its sting in his eyes. Panting, he rounded beneath the looming shadow of the crag—and then, a matter of scant yards ahead, the mountain showed still another mood.

The gentle slope came to an abrupt end. Beyond, plunging steep for almost a thousand feet, ran the scree channel —for all the world like a stationary river of tiny rocks and pebbles, a broad, deep band of gravel-sized rubble studded here and there with the occasional stone of larger dimensions.

Millan jumped.

Behind, Thane slowed. Then, as the wild figure below continued its mad progress, running, jumping, body upright, heels digging as they ploughed the crunching pebbles, he followed.

When you scree-run, you move fast—faster than any other human being on two feet. Each jumping step propelled Thane five to six feet outwards—but a skidding twenty feet downwards as his boots contacted the yielding pebbles. Arms wide to maintain balance, he plunged on, a rustling storm of gravel following in his wake.

Ahead, Millan's frantic progress caused similar miniature avalanches, while two rising dust-plumes marked the trail of their joint descent. For either man to stop now would mean to lose. The mountain slopes appeared blurred now, and the scree grew steeper, until they were sliding down the occasional acute-angled pitch.

Slide—jump—run—jump— Millan's dust-trail crossed Thane's path for a brief second. Just long enough to obscure his pursuer's view, blind him to the smooth, heart-shaped rock, lying loose among the surrounding gravel. Thane's toe stubbed hard. He overbalanced forward, felt his other foot bog down in the yielding scree, and then he fell headlong, skidding fifteen yards onwards before he came to a standstill.

Dazed, shaken, he looked up, then froze at the scene below.

Millan was still running, unaware of what had happened. But behind him, moving almost lazily, no bigger than a man's head, the heart-shaped rock was beginning to roll. It gathered pace, and company . . . now a small wave of scree was on the move, travelling with deceptively slow acceleration, while on ahead the heart-shaped rock danced a zigzag path, fast closing the distance between it and the man below.

Above, Thane bellowed a warning.

Almost drowned by the rumbling scree, the shout still registered in Millan's ears. Sliding, about to jump again, he half-turned, saw the rock taking a final, bouncing curve towards him, and did the only thing left . . . threw himself into a sideways roll.

The heart-shaped boulder flew above him and kept on its downward path. But for Millan, the dive for safety still spelled disaster. On he spun, arms and legs waving in a futile attempt to brake his own momentum, scree-dust rising, a torrent of gravel following in his wake. Three hundred feet below, where the scree-course levelled into a broad, flat bed, the man finally rolled to a halt, the pursuing pebbles rattling against his still, battered form.

Fifteen minutes later, after a torturous, crunching descent, Thane reached his side.

Clothes ripped and dust-covered, arms and legs half-buried in gravel, face torn and bloodied, Erick Millan was still alive, but unconscious.

The Chief Inspector took out a handkerchief and wiped some of the fine dust and grit from around his quarry's nose and mouth.

Then he sat down, and lit a cigarette.

By dusk, the rescue party had them back at Glenmore. Phil Moss, perky beneath the white bandage swathing his forehead, his left leg heavily splinted, was on the first stretcher to be lifted into the ambulance. Millan, conscious now, but drowsy under a massive pain-killing injection of morphia, was on the second. Two uniformed County police climbed in after them, the ambulance doors closed, and the vehicle growled to life, heading back down the Aviemore Road.

Thane turned to where Sergeant MacNeil and Constable Donny Stewart were waiting, and grinned.

"Sergeant!"

MacNeil stiffened.

"I could use a drink—and that's an order."

They piled into the police car, and set off in the ambulance's wake.

Two days later, in the antiseptically cheerful atmosphere of an orthopaedic ward at Glasgow Western Infirmary, Phil Moss sat up in bed and complained. "I tell you, Colin, the whole thing's a plot—'rest here till the end of the week' says the doctor. Then starts asking questions about my ulcer, my diet, how would I like an X ray, do I know they've got a first-class specialist in that sort of thing." He growled. "I know what they're after, but they're not on. No hospital's getting me on their operating table so some bunch of medical students can have a conducted tour of my innards." A narrow strip of white plaster covered the gash on his forehead. The bedclothes bulked with the shape of the heavy plaster cast on his leg.

"You were lucky, Phil." Thane helped himself to another grape from the dish on the bedside locker. "Doc Williams had a word with the orthopaedic surgeon—that hunk of granite could have landed you with a nastily complicated compound fracture, but it's a clean break. A month off duty, and you'll be more or less as good as new."

"Uh-huh." Moss eased himself into a more comfortable position. "What's the latest on the Millans?"

"Erick's all right. He looked a mess, but he got off almost as lightly as you did. Two broken ribs and a smashed elbow. They strapped him up enough to push him through court this morning, and about now he should be in the prison hospital block at Barlinnie. Old Ludd—well—" the Chief Inspector shook his head. "He's in the remand wing up there, of course. Completely withdrawn from everything around him. It's not an act, and he isn't going insane. He just doesn't care."

"I feel almost sorry for him," mused Moss.

"Sorry? Maybe, Phil—but remember Sammy Bell. He laid him down on a road and ran a car over him twice. And but for some little drops of blood that pointed the wrong way we might never have known it was murder."

"Well, they'll each draw an automatic life sentence," said Moss, moving the grapes a little further distant from his visitor. "Maybe even serve it together."

Thane shook his head. "No. Buddha and I had a talk about that. He says that once they've been sentenced he can fix it so they're kept apart. I can't imagine either of them disagreeing with that move." He got up from the bed. "Time I was moving. While you're relaxing in here the rest of us still have to work. Anyway," his eyes twinkled. "There's another visitor waiting—in fact, here she comes now."

Cherry-stalk hat bobbing, Ida Murdock moved purpose-fully down the ward towards them, a large basket of grapes clutched tight in one hand.

"Oh no!" groaned Phil.

But when you're in bed, wearing hospital pyjamas and a half-hundredweight plaster cast, there's no place left to hide.